Shake Me to Wake Me

The Best Short Fiction of
Stan Nicholls

Shake Me to Wake Me

The Best Short Fiction of

Stan Nicholls

NewCon Press
England

First edition, published in the UK November 2013
by NewCon Press

NCP59 Paperback

10 9 8 7 6 5 4 3 2 1

Cover art by Ben Baldwin
Cover design by Andy Bigwood

Minimal editorial interference by Ian Whates
Text layout by Storm Constantine

Printed in the UK by Berforts Information Press

Contents

For Mia Rose Fifer, with all my love.

Sleeping With the Writer

An Introduction

"Nobody ever sleeps with the writer to get on a picture."
— *Hollywood saying*

That's true. You must have heard writers, whatever their medium, complaining about being at the bottom of the food chain. But forget that and think about the sleeping bit. Because sleeping is when we dream.

For want of a more accurate term, the majority of the stories in this collection fall into the category of speculative fiction. "What if" stories, if you prefer. But whatever the tag, the paradox about short stories is that everybody says they love them but nobody buys them, unless they happen to be by one of a handful of hugely popular writers.

This is baffling, particularly in the context of speculative fiction. Short stories were the backbone of the science fiction and supernatural genres. Perhaps that wasn't so much the case in respect of fantasy, of the heroic or epic kind, though there are notable exceptions, like Robert E. Howard and Fritz Leiber.

Science fiction emerged as a discrete category from the American pulp magazines that began publishing in the 1920's. In fact, the letter columns of the pulps gave rise to the first fan groups, seeding the worldwide sf community. The horror pulps, notably *Weird Tales*, played a similar role.

The influence of the shorter form in sf carried on through the golden age of the '40's and '50's, the '60's New Wave, the cyberpunk 80's and right down to the present, where the print magazines are few and their readerships are dwindling.

Some writers contend that writing a short story is harder than writing a novel. That only holds true if you see short stories as truncated novels. But if a novel is a door to another world, a short story is a keyhole. Consequently, the writing requires a different approach, and often a different style.

Short stories and novels are closely enough related that if they tried to marry they'd be arrested for incest. Related, but different. Both in terms of their creation and their consumption. For readers, shorts are achievable; a reasonable investment of time. It's the same for authors; writing a novel is a mental marathon, whereas a short story is a sprint with the finish line in view. Between the slog of novels it's refreshing to tackle something that takes a fraction of the effort.

But the main reason writers are drawn to short stories is basically because they've had a short story idea. Some ideas lend themselves to novels, others to shorts. For proof of that, think of the novels you've read that came over like a stretched short idea. Or the shorts you wish had been expanded into a novel. So it's important that when evaluating an idea, writers choose the appropriate length, and accordingly the appropriate approach and style.

I had to make some hard choices when selecting the stories for this collection. My output of shorts hasn't been great - somewhere between forty and fifty over quite a long period - but I still put a lot of thought into which ones to include. In the end I simply settled for the ones I personally liked the most, and which I think came nearest to what I set out to achieve.

Something else I agonised over was whether to bring the stories up to date. I mean in terms of some of the minor elements. In the end I decided I would. So characters now use mobile phones instead of telephone boxes, digital cameras instead of developing their own photos, MP3 players instead of a Walkman. I did this because I didn't want readers stumbling over anachronisms. Fortunately none of the plots rely on any of these things. I also did a little rewriting and smoothing here and there.

The first two stories, "Softies" and "Picking Up The Tab", were written for the young adult market. It's possible you might not have known that if I hadn't told you, given that everyone working in that field tries not to break the first rule: don't write down to your readership. In many ways young adults are the hardest readers to write for.

What are the hardest genres? Humour and horror. It's too easy to write laughable horror and humour that comes over as gruesome. "Throwing A Wobbly" and "Polly Put The Mockers On" are attempts at humour. You decide whether they merit screams of mirth or derision. All I'll say is that, considering when "Throwing A Wobbly" was written, I'm pleased to have pointed to a topic that's since become a pressing social problem.

"We Are For The Dark" is the only story here that isn't speculative in the same sense as the others. It's a crime story and, unusually for me, it has a historical setting. Although in terms of the "What if" aspect, speculative may not be that inaccurate a label.

"SPOIL" is concerned with religion. A contentious subject at the best of times, yet some of the most positive reactions I got were from people of faith. That pleased me because I wrote it to be read both ways, if you know what I mean.

The trio of stories with the umbrella title "Three Whimsies" came about in a slightly unusual way. In 2000 I had the privilege of being one of the guests of honour at UK's Fantasycon. A couple of weeks before the event I got a call from the organisers saying they'd reserved a chunk of the programme book for something by me, preferably original. Could I let them have it as soon as possible, please? I was knee deep in a novel at the time. Like a lot of writers I keep ideas books. Flipping through them for inspiration, I fished out three brief sets of notes that I intended, one day, to work up into shorts. Unable to decide which one to go for, I tackled all three, writing fast and in a style somewhat different to my usual approach. I think the result was actually better than if I'd handled them in a more conventional way.

"Juice" is, I suppose, an urban fantasy, if we have to brand it. It's possibly the most 'What iffy' story here. "The Gripes of Wrath" was written especially for this collection. It's fiction. Mostly.

These days, short fiction in all genres survives and thrives, apart, of course, from the ubiquitous Internet, in small and independent presses. So let's hear it for Ian Whates and NewCon Press for keeping the spirit of shorts alive. And that's not an alcoholic pun.

Are you ready to dream with open eyes? It's not going to get you into the movies, but I hope you like the pictures.

Stan Nicholls
July 2013

Softies

It was like this.

The boy wore a green baseball cap, blue jeans, black Nikes with white flashes and a T-shirt carrying the legend *Gravity – Don't take it for granted.* The headphones of an MP3 player pressed snugly against the stems of his gold-framed shades.

The bear wore only a red silk ribbon tied in a floppy bow at his throat.

As they stepped off the bus at the shopping mall a breeze ruffled the bear's artificial yellow-orange fur. He wrinkled his snout and growled softly. The boy glanced at him and upped his music's volume from tinny hiss to rhythmic buzz.

None of the other shoppers paid any attention.

Teenage boy and teenage bear strolled into a clothing store. After browsing for a while the boy noticed a middle-aged security guard staring suspiciously at them from the other side of the sales floor. The bear saw him too, and his unblinking, black button eyes briefly flared. The guard looked away.

The pair emerged clutching plastic carrier bags, and the boy made for a rack of shirts outside another, adjoining clothes shop. The bear stood to one side for a moment as he clacked the hangers, then lumbered over and tugged his arm. The boy checked his watch. Grinning, he playfully back-handed the bear's massive barrel chest.

Side by side, they set off in the direction of the town centre, the boy breaking step only to tease a fresh stick of gum from his hip pocket. Outside the sports complex the pavement narrowed and they had to walk single-file to make way for a woman and her Companion. The couple were deep in conversation, but the woman nodded politely at the boy before returning her attention to the pink polka dot giraffe loping along beside her.

A small bell round the giraffe's neck tinkled, the sound following boy and bear until they reached an intersection and it was drowned by traffic.

They crossed the road hand in paw.

Piers hated wedding receptions.

Hated the crowds and the din. Hated the grotesque drunks and their rambling speeches. Hated the insincere greetings exchanged by people who couldn't stand the sight of each other. And on this occasion hated being the one sent to cover the event for *The Journal.*

Admittedly he was in a bad mood when he arrived, still smarting at Mr T's refusal to come with him. These days the atmosphere always seemed tense at home and it was starting to interfere with Piers' work. Not that he was enjoying the job much right now. His editor insisted on assigning him to an endless round of fetes, christenings, supermarket openings; anything but the story Piers really wanted to write. Assuming it *was* a story.

He abandoned his cardboard plate of tasteless food in the debris on the buffet table, remembering the old saying about how an angry man couldn't tell if he was eating boiled cabbage or stewed umbrella.

There was no need to stay. He had a few slurred quotes from the bridegroom, Alan Richards – a minor local celebrity since joining a second division football club – and knew he should get back to the office. But he couldn't face it yet.

A cheer went up at the far end of the hall as a group of revellers showered each other with spray from shaken lager cans. Someone started banging discordantly on the keys of an upright piano. A ragged chorus of *My Way* rose to add to the racket. Piers winced.

'Drink, sir?'

Startled, he turned. A panda holding a tray of polystyrene cups was standing behind him.

As Piers took in the ill-fitting waiter's costume he was hit by the thought that the sight was more than faintly ridiculous. And in a strange way, shaming. The notion was completely alien, but somehow heightened his feeling that there was something going on he didn't understand.

He found it impossible to meet the panda's passive gaze as he reached for an orange juice. Some of the juice splashed into the tray and against the waiter's rubber palm, and he directed a mumbled apology at the Companion's departing back. Draining the cup, Piers elbowed his way to fresh air.

Outside, the sun was beginning to set. A photographer, anxious for a few last shots, fussed around the bride and groom. The bridesmaids, four dolls dressed in frothy blue gowns, golden wire wool hair piled beehive-style, giggled together in a corner. Two pageboys nibbled chunks of wedding cake on a nearby bench.

A fleeting blast of noise and light burst from the hall. A young man stepped out, blinking, his jacket draped over one shoulder. In his free hand he held a black plastic object roughly the size of a paperback. Piers instinctively patted his side pockets, found them empty and smiled sheepishly. The young man came over.

'I think this is yours.'

Piers accepted the portable tape recorder, slipping its strap around his left wrist.

'Thanks. I've lost more of these than you've –'

'Been to lousy wedding receptions?'

They laughed.

'I suppose it is pretty gruesome,' Piers said.

'You're a journalist, aren't you?'

'Yeah.' He held out his hand. 'Piers Kennedy. I'm with *The Journal.*'

'Matthew Richards, Mr Kennedy. The groom's my uncle.'

'Call me Piers. Any plans to follow him into professional football, Matt?'

'No way!' He gave his jacket a shake, began putting it on. 'As a matter of fact, I'd like to be a reporter.'

'So I'm talking to a potential rival, am I?'

Matt flicked a strand of jet black hair from his forehead, slightly nervously Piers thought, and he regretted teasing him.

'Only kidding. But the usual advice I give anybody wanting to go into journalism is, *'Don't.'* It's nowhere near as glamorous as most people think.' Noting Matt's frown, he added quickly, 'Mind you, that's what *I* was told. You leaving now?'

'Yes.' He nodded at the hall. 'I've had enough of that for one day. I'm just going to pick up my Companion. How about you?'

'Er, mine's not with me.' The memory of Mr T's unreasonable behaviour flooded back, along with Piers' irritation. 'He had to stay at home. I'll walk over with you, though.'

Naturally the Companions had a separate hall; in this case a large, rather shabby wooden hut well away from the main building. Matt barged straight in. Piers followed, and it took him a few seconds to adjust to the gloom inside.

What he saw chilled him.

The place was full of Companions. Dolls, pandas, teddies. Grey-furred koalas, dwarf trolls with shocks of green hair, woolly gorillas. Further back, in the shadows, hulking, indistinct shapes he couldn't identify. There was nothing unusual about this. What was spooky was the *silence*. And the fact that every Companion in the room was absolutely still, like figures in a waxworks. Piers wondered if they were always like this when people weren't around. Or whether they had frozen at his and Matt's unexpected entrance, as though caught planning some mischief or conspiracy.

It was an absurd idea. At least, it would have been until recently. Now Piers wasn't so sure.

Matt seemed equally affected by the scene. He stood awkwardly in the doorway, lost for words. Piers touched his arm.

'Matt?'

'Oh. Yeah.' He took a step forward and peered into the

murk. 'Rufus?'

For the space of three heartbeats, nothing happened. Then a bear near the front turned his huge head their way.

Very, very slowly.

As soon as he did so, all the others turned as well, just as unhurriedly. Scores of eyes regarded the humans. Cold eyes.

Piers had never felt so uncomfortable in the presence of Companions before. It was as though he had interrupted something intensely private, and was despised for it.

Matt broke the spell. 'Come on, Rufus. We're going.'

The bear's lips twisted into a copy of a smile. There was no warmth in it. 'Yes, Matthew. Of course.' There was no emotion in the guttural voice either.

They walked to the street together. No one spoke. Before they parted, Piers wrote his telephone number on a scrap of paper and gave it to Matt. He told him to call if he wanted to talk about his ambition to be a journalist. Piers liked him, but that wasn't the only reason he did it. He guessed Matt was having a problem with Rufus. Maybe it was similar to the one Piers had with Mr T.

Or perhaps both of them were trapped in something much bigger.

At his car, fumbling for the keys, he chanced to look up. Matt and his Companion were moving away, but the bear was staring back at Piers over his shoulder. He wore an expression of pure, savage hatred.

Piers shuddered.

'You don't think we've overdone it with the flowers, do you?'

'Stop *fussing*, Jerry; everything's lovely.' Cora pointed to the chair next to her bed. 'Come and sit down. Calm yourself.'

She returned her attention to their baby. Cradled snugly, the child was sucking her mother's little finger.

Jerry did as he was told and sat, but couldn't stop fidgeting. For the hundredth time he scanned the hospital room. Then his eyes darted to the clock on the bedside table.

'They'll be here any time now.'

Cora smiled and reached for his hand. 'I know, dear. And it's going to be all right. Don't worry.'

There was a double rap at the door. Jerry leapt up, nervously straightened his tie, and went to open it.

A small but impressive group shuffled in. They were led by a doctor in a white coat. Next came a smartly dressed man with a briefcase. After him, a nurse, wheeling a cot containing a bundle wrapped in a pink shawl. A doll followed, clasping a bouquet of roses. Finally, stooping slightly to avoid the top of the door frame, a bear.

The room suddenly seemed a lot smaller.

Greetings and introductions over, the cot was pushed to the end of Cora's bed and everyone formed a semi-circle.

The smartly dressed man opened a small leather-bound book, cleared his throat and began to read.

'We are gathered here to celebrate the bonding of this child...' he inclined his head toward the baby '... and this Companion...' a dip in the direction of the cot

'... as friends, consorts and soul-mates for as long as they both shall live.'

He gently lifted the baby from Cora's arms. 'Let it be known that from this day forward Karen Grace Taylor is bound to her Companion in the eyes of the Law.'

Handing the baby to the nurse, he looked down at the cot. 'And that henceforth this Companion –' He faltered and turned to Jerry.

'Crystal,' Jerry said.

'– this Companion, Crystal,' the official continued, 'shall serve, support and protect her charge at all times. I declare this child and this Companion bonded.' He closed the book and offered Cora and Jerry his congratulations.

A polite round of applause echoed him. But Jerry noticed that Vanda the doll and Chad the bear, he and Cora's

Companions, didn't join in.

The smartly dressed man snapped open his briefcase, pulled out a sheet of paper and handed it to Jerry. 'The final legal formality, Mr Taylor,' he explained.

Jerry signed the document and passed it back. It was witnessed by the nurse after she placed the baby in the cot next to its Companion. Mr and Mrs Taylor thanked everyone and they all trooped out.

Alone again, they embraced. 'It was wonderful,' Cora said, her eyes dewy. 'Karen's going to be looked after and loved by all three of us now.'

In the cot, the tiny panda stirred and let out a squeaky bleat, like a young lamb. It wriggled closer to baby Karen and placed a little furry arm around her. Jerry and Cora beamed.

It was the happiest day of their lives.

It was the unhappiest day of Piers' life.

Teds could be grumpy, everybody knew that, but Mr T's moods were getting him down. And what really made Piers angry was that he didn't know why his Companion was acting this way. Hadn't he always been kind to Mr T? Shown him every consideration? Been there when he needed him?

The bear was out in the garden, skulking around miserably as usual, but Piers had made up his mind to confront him when he came in. This thing had to be cleared up.

The back door slammed.

Mr T walked into the living room and slouched on the sofa without a word. Piers was strangely uneasy in his presence, a feeling he had never had with his Companion until just a few weeks ago, when all this moodiness began. He sighed.

'Come on, what's wrong?' he asked.

No reply.

He tried again. 'Look, if I've done anything to upset you, I'm sorry. Can't we talk about it? Please?'

The bear seemed to notice him for the first time. 'You

wouldn't understand.'

'Try me.'

'Have you ever wondered what it's like to be a Companion?'

Piers was surprised by the question. It didn't make sense. 'What do you mean?'

'It hasn't occurred to you that I might have a mind of my own, has it? That I'm sick of always doing what you want, going where you want to go, being what you want me to be.'

Even more puzzling. Companions just didn't talk this way.

'You've got a good life here, haven't you?' Piers said. 'I don't see the problem.' It came out rather more sharply than he intended, and he could see the bear's anger rising.

'I said you wouldn't understand.' Mr T got up and plodded to the door.

Piers reached him as he was turning the handle. He put one hand over the bear's paw, the other on his burly forearm. 'Don't go. I'll try to understand, Mr Thumpy. Just –'

'Take your filthy hands off me.'

The words were quietly spoken, but filled with as much menace as if they had been bellowed. They were like a slap in the face to Piers. He let go and backed off.

The bear's eyes bored into him. His voice was higher now, more intense. 'And don't you ever, *ever*, call me by that stupid name again.'

Piers was startled and confused. For the first time he realised what a big, powerful creature Mr T was. It amazed him that he had never been aware of it before. As his life-long Companion towered over him, his face a mask of fury, Piers saw him in a totally new light. That frightened him.

Time slowed to a snail's pace as they faced each other, motionless, neither speaking.

The telephone warbled.

It snapped Piers out of his trance. He retreated clumsily, banging a low table with the back of his knees and sending a lamp flying. Ignoring it, his eyes fixed on Mr T, he scrabbled for the receiver on his desk.

The bear remained at the door, radiating malice.

'Hello?' Piers realised his voice sounded tinny and breathless.

'Piers? Is that you?' His caller sounded pretty shaken himself.

'Who is this?'

'It's me. Matt. Matthew Richards. We met at –'

'I remember.' He glanced at Mr T. 'This isn't a good time, Matt. Perhaps –'

'I need your help, Piers. Something... *bad's* happened to Rufus. There's nobody else I can –'

'Okay, take it easy. Give me the address.' He scribbled it on the pad, tossed the pen aside. 'Right. I'll be there as soon as I can.'

When he got off the phone, Mr T had gone.

As he drove to Matt's house, Piers tried to make sense of what was happening. Mr T was acting completely out of character. There were the stories he'd heard about other people's Companions and *their* odd behaviour. And now Matt was having trouble with Rufus. Could all these things be connected? If they were, how?

He arrived at the address he had been given in time to see two men in green overalls carrying a stretcher out of the house. Rufus, head and right arm bandaged, was lying on it, eyes closed. At the pavement end of the garden path, Matt held the gate open for them. Piers got out of the car and hurried over.

'Oh, Piers. Thanks for coming.' Matt looked relieved to see him. His face was chalky white.

They watched as the stretcher was slipped into the back of the transporter. The doors were closed, revealing the words COMPANIONS RECOVERY SERVICE in large red letters, then the attendants clambered into the front seats. The van took off with siren wailing.

'I'm sorry to drag you over here, Piers, but my parents are

away and –'

Piers cut him off with a wave of his hand. 'It's all right. Just tell me what happened.'

'Rufus was attacked.'

'*Attacked?*'

'Yeah, by a gang of thugs, right here outside the house.'

'How is he?'

'They say he's going to be okay. But he's pretty shaken up.'

'So are you. Let's go inside and talk about this.'

Sitting at the kitchen table, sipping a mug of strong, sweet tea, some of the colour returned to Matt's face.

'Now, let me get this straight,' Piers said. 'Rufus was beaten-up by a bunch of hooligans ...?'

'Yes.'

'How come they picked on him?'

'Can't say. He probably gave them some mouth. I always tell him to ignore those sort of idiots, but he's been really grumpy lately.'

That struck a chord with Piers.

'Anyway,' Matt went on, 'the first I knew about it was when I heard this terrific disturbance outside. When I got out there they were running off. Mind you, they did catch one of them.'

'Really?'

'Yeah. My sister, Emma, was here at the time and she called the police. They picked him up a couple of blocks away.'

'Where's your sister now?'

'She went out just before you got here. Her Companion was a bit cut up about it all. She's a doll, and you know what *they* can be like.' He made a sour face and Piers smiled. 'Emma took her for a walk.'

'Do you know where the police are holding this guy?'

'Princes Street, I think.'

'Good.' He took out his mobile.

Piers knew a Detective Sergeant called Hopkins at Princes Street police station. When he got there, he was surprised when Hopkins said he could see Nicholas Barker, the arrested man.

'You don't normally let journalists interview prisoners,' Piers commented.

'Well,' Hopkins replied, 'he isn't actually a prisoner. We're not charging him.'

'Why not?'

'No witnesses. He's one of the gang that had a go at that Companion. Got to be. But there's nothing we can do without proof. We're just checking if he's wanted for anything else before letting him go.'

'Why should he speak to me?'

'Because you're the Press. He wants some publicity for his ideas about Companions. Really down on them, he is.'

'You've no doubt Barker was involved?'

'I'm sure of it.' The sergeant frowned. 'We're getting more and more reports about attacks like this all the time. Some of them very serious. And, as you know, the most we can do these people for is damage to property. But then, assaulting a Companion's not the same as assaulting a human, is it?'

Sergeant Hopkins took Piers to an interview room and left him with the suspect.

Barker was a picture of arrogance. He sat on a chair balanced on its back legs, his feet on the table, hands laced behind his neck.

'You're that reporter bloke, aren't you?'

'That's right, and I haven't got much time. I just want to ask you a couple of questions.' Piers flipped open his notebook.

'Ask away.'

'Why did you attack that Companion today?'

'You can't prove I did, and neither can the cops.'

'Let me put it another way then. What do you think about him being attacked?'

Barker grinned crookedly. 'Oh well, if it's an *opinion* you want, that's different. I think it served him right.'

'Why?'

'I hate the parasites. Idle, they are, and stupid. Dead stupid. Makes me flesh creep, the way they slobber over you, always getting under your feet. And they smell, you know, some of 'em. Who needs it?'

'If you feel that way, how do you get on with *your* Companion?'

'Haven't got one.'

Piers was shocked. He knew there were people who didn't have Companions, usually those disabled in mind or body and unable to cope, and even they were very rare. Boasting of not having a Companion was something Piers had never come across before. It was like saying you'd cut off your right arm and being proud of it. He almost felt sorry for Barker. But only almost.

'Why haven't you got a Companion?'

'Got rid of him, didn't I? Ted, he was. Useless object. Took him down the town hall and told 'em I didn't want him no more.'

'What did they do with him?'

'Dunno.'

'Don't you care? '

'*No!* If me and me mates had our way, there wouldn't be no Companions.'

'Where would they go?'

'Search me. Dump 'em on a desert island, chuck 'em down a coal mine. Better yet, shoot the lot of 'em. They're not wanted.'

'And you think it's okay to use violence against them?'

'I don't know nothing about no violence. But so what if a few Companions get a good kickin'?'

Before Piers could answer, the door opened. Sergeant Hopkins came in.

'All right, Barker, you're clear. Off you go. Don't let me see you in here again.'

Barker smirked, righted his chair with a crash and kicked it aside. He thrust his hands into his trouser pockets and swaggered over to Piers. 'You tell people about them dirty Companions, right? You tell 'em –'

'*Mister* Barker,' Hopkins interrupted, 'I suggest you do with your mouth what you've done with your mind – close it. Now, *out!*'

The Royal Infirmary for Companions was a run-down old building Piers had never visited before, and he got lost twice in the endless corridors before coming to the dormitory Rufus was in. The bear was propped-up in a large iron-framework bed. Matt was sitting beside him, along with a young woman Piers didn't know.

Matt brightened when he saw him. 'Hello, Piers. This is Emma, my sister. Emma, this is Piers, the journalist I told you about.'

The girl leaned over and shook his hand. 'Hi. Thanks for coming.'

They all looked at Rufus.

'And how's the patient?' Piers wanted to know.

'He's fine,' offered Emma.

'Oh yes, fine,' Rufus said bitterly. 'Insulted, beaten-up on the street, treated like –'

'For goodness sake!' Matt cut in. 'You're not badly hurt. And at least the police got one of them.'

'Ah,' said Piers. 'I'm afraid they had to let him go.'

Emma was outraged. '*What?*'

'No evidence, apparently.'

'Surprise, surprise,' Rufus grumbled. 'One law for us Companions and another for you humans. As usual.'

Matt was obviously embarrassed at the bear's rudeness. 'Have you got time for a coffee, Piers?'

'Sure. 'Bye, Emma. Nice to meet you. 'Bye, Rufus. Take care.'

The bear ignored him.

They didn't make it to the cafeteria. Outside the ward they bumped into a grey-haired man in a green tunic. Matt introduced him as Dr Reynolds, the medic in charge of Rufus' case. Piers asked the doctor how many Companions were brought in after being attacked.

'Far too many, Mr Kennedy, and the number's increasing all the time.'

'How long's this been going on?'

'It started building-up about a year ago, I'd say. Before that, almost every Companion we saw here had been in an accident of some sort. Just occasionally, we'd get one injured by his human during a row, but they were really unusual.'

'And now?'

'Now we're seeing this kind of thing almost every week. Organised attacks. And nobody seems to be taking them seriously.'

As if on cue, a trolley was wheeled past bearing a furry red chimp. Her left leg was missing.

'There's an example,' Dr Reynolds said. 'They brought her in last night. In fact, you'll have to excuse me now. I'm part of the repair team.'

He trotted off to catch up with the trolley.

'You're a pain in the butt, Kennedy.'

Murray Baxter, editor of *The Journal*, was not known for mincing his words. Piers, fists clenched in frustration, sat in Baxter's office and suffered the lecture in silence.

'You come in here,' the boss added, 'with a crazy story about Companions doing weird things and gangs of toughs roaming the streets, and expect me to believe you.'

'I can prove it, chief.'

'You can't. All you've got is a few comments from some sawbones and what you call a hunch. Well, let me tell you, young man –'

One of the many telephones on Baxter's vast desk rang. He snatched it, yelled '*Not now!*' and slammed it down again. He carried on as though nothing had happened. 'Let me tell you that when you've been in this business as many years as I have, *then* I'll start listening to your so-called hunches.' He pushed his glasses back up the bridge of his nose.

'Maybe I haven't got any cast-iron proof, but something's going on. I know it.'

'Really? *What?*' Baxter snorted.

'I think things are breaking down. Between us and the Companions, that is.'

'Nonsense!' his editor roared. 'Just look at me and Troy.' He jerked his thumb at the ageing panda sprawled on a settee by the wall. 'Fifty-eight years together and never a cross word. Isn't that right, Troy?'

'That's right, Murray, never a cross word,' his Companion confirmed. 'Through thick and thin,' he croaked. 'Good times and –'

'Thank you, Troy, that'll do,' Baxter told him.

Piers thought about how some humans and their Companions grew to look and act like each other. Baxter and Troy were classic examples. He bit his lip to stop himself laughing.

Baxter brought his fist down on the desk. 'Humans and Companions have always been together and always will be! It's the natural way of things and nothing's going to change it!'

'Supposing I could come up with evidence? Something you couldn't ignore?'

The editor slumped back in his chair. 'Do that, Kennedy, and I'll take you seriously. But I very much doubt you can.'

Another phone rang. Baxter picked it up and barked, 'Just a minute!' He put a hand over the mouthpiece. 'Close the door on your way out.'

Piers slammed it.

In the spacious newsroom outside, several reporters were studying some photographs. He wandered over.

'Hi, Jim, Dave. What's up?'

Jim tossed over a photograph. It showed a car that had

crashed into a wall. A human arm could just be seen poking out in front of it.

'Odd one, this,' Jim said. 'Woman stops her car outside her house and goes to open the garage door. Leaves her Companion sitting in the passenger seat with the engine running. Next thing, the car shoots forward and crushes her.'

'How?'

'There didn't seem to be a mechanical fault. Best guess is that her Companion got itself tangled with the accelerator in some way. Sad. But just one of those bizarre accidents, you know?'

'Yes,' Piers said thoughtfully, 'I suppose so.'

The fireman wiped sweat from his forehead with the back of his arm. He leaned against the cab of the engine and clicked on the radio handset.

'Hello, sir? Yes, we've got it under control now.'

He scanned the smouldering ruin. The front door of the house hung at a crazy angle, black smoke billowing from inside. A stream of water flowed over the doorstep and into the garden. Two other firemen jogged past holding a ladder.

'What?' He put a hand over one ear so he could hear better. 'Yes, I'm afraid so, sir. Three deaths that we know of. Two adults and a child. Name of Taylor. Didn't stand a chance. The house is completely gutted.'

An ambulance pulled away noisily, blue light flashing.

He had to shout into the microphone. 'The amazing thing, sir, is that their Companions got out. Yes, not a mark on them.'

He moved to allow someone to pass.

'No, they haven't a clue how it started. Say they were woken up by the fumes and just managed to escape before the place went up. Yes, they were. *Very* lucky.'

He felt really sorry for the bedraggled Companions standing over by the police car. Funny, but they didn't seem to be taking it too badly. He supposed it was the shock. They looked quite pathetic though, wrapped in red blankets, their faces streaked with soot and grime.

A bear, and a doll with a baby panda in her arms.

'So that's how it stands. If I can come up with proof, my editor will give me time for some serious investigation.'

'What kind of proof?' Matt asked.

'That I don't know,' Piers admitted gloomily.

A waitress arrived and served them with two cups of coffee. It was raining and the cafe was nearly empty. Piers stared through the window at the traffic crawling by outside.

Neither of them spoke for a moment. Then Matt said, 'Something peculiar happened today.'

'Yeah?'

'It may not mean anything, of course.'

'Go on.'

'When I was coming back from the infirmary with Rufus, another bear came up to us in the street. Or up to Rufus, rather. I hadn't seen him before.'

'And?'

'They stood talking for a while,' Matt said, 'then this other bear passed something to Rufus. They didn't think I saw, but I did.'

'What was it?'

'A small piece of folded paper. Rufus scrunched it in his paw, and I didn't say anything. Then, this afternoon, I found it in the waste bin in the living room. It was torn in half and screwed up.'

'Have you got it?'

'Yes.' Matt put his hand in his jacket pocket. 'Here it is. I taped it back together. Doesn't make much sense though.'

He laid it on the table and smoothed it down. It was a perfectly ordinary-looking sheet of notepaper, torn from a lined pad. All it had written on it, in blue ink, was a *12*, followed by the words *17 Gance*. Piers rested his elbows on the table, chin in palms, and studied it.

Suddenly his eyes lit up and he slapped the plastic table-top. 'Got it!'

Matt was puzzled. 'What do you think it means?'

'It's that word Gance. A very unusual name. There's a place down by the river called Gance Road. Suppose it's an address – 17 Gance Road?'

'And the 12?'

'That could be a time. Rufus was handed it this afternoon, right? After midday?'

'Yeah.'

'It probably means midnight then.'

'So it's a time and a place for –'

'*A meeting!*' they exclaimed together.

'It has to be, Matt. Let's assume it's tonight. I'm going to be there.'

'Not without me, you're not,' Matt told him.

They parked two streets away and walked to Gance Road. It was a rough part of town and few of the street lights were working. But a full moon lit their way.

When Matt told Piers that Rufus had slipped out of the house, thinking Matt and Emma were asleep, Piers knew they were on to something.

He looked at his watch. 11.55. They had to get a move on.

Number seventeen turned out to be an abandoned warehouse on a derelict street. A light flickered in one of the lower windows, then as quickly went out. Piers and Matt decided it would be unwise to try the front door. They crept around to the back. Matt discovered a smaller window secured only by two rotting pieces of wood.

They quietly climbed in.

A small, empty room, covered in years of dust. Piers padded over to the door and cautiously opened it. There was a corridor beyond. At the end of it, another door, which creaked noisily.

Afraid someone would hear them, they waited a moment.

They were on a landing. A wooden barrier, about four feet tall, faced them. Stooping, they went to it and gingerly peeped over.

The scene below took their breath away.

It was an immense cellar. Softly glowing oil lamps were scattered around the place. A makeshift platform, built from packing cases, occupied one end.

Scores of Companions of every kind, possibly a hundred or more, filled all the available space. They stood, they sat, they leaned against the shadowy walls or huddled together in groups.

And, as on the day of the wedding, they were mute and immobile.

It was so deathly quiet, Piers feared the crowd could hear his heart beating. Very carefully he removed the lens cap from the infra-red camera hanging around his neck. He lifted the camera and looked through the view-finder. But he didn't dare risk clicking the shutter. Then there was a flurry of movement at the front of the gathering and Piers had another shock.

Rufus walked on to the stage.

Matt's fingers dug into Piers' arm. Piers prayed he wouldn't do anything impulsive and expose them.

Rufus raised his arms and the silence was broken. A great roar went up. Piers took advantage of it and rapidly snapped half a dozen photographs.

The clamour suddenly stopped. Rufus addressed the crowd.

'Brothers and sisters! The time of our deliverance draws near!'

Another round of cheers and muffled claps from leathery paws.

'We have suffered long enough! The humans demand our love, our devotion, our obedience! What do they give us in return? Contempt! What rights do we have? The rights of property, of owned things!'

Uproar from the audience. Piers took another batch of

photos.

'Are we not as they in our hearts? If they wound us with their tongues, do we not grieve? If they prick us, do we not cry out? If they cut us, does our stuffing not flow?'

He was answered with shouts of, *'Yes! Yes!'*

'As some of you know,' Rufus said, his voice lowering, 'I have recently suffered at their hands myself.'

A Companion yelled, 'Shame!' There was a rumble of agreement.

'Yes, I suffered. And I suffered doubly. They robbed me of my dignity, and would have robbed me of my life. Yet those responsible are not to be punished.'

His voice rose again. 'We cannot look to our masters for justice! The only justice we can expect is that which we take for ourselves! Some brothers and sisters are beginning to strike for freedom! Join them! Cast off your chains!'

Bedlam. Companions whooped, screamed, cheered and shrieked. They stamped their feet, hooves and paws. A chant broke out.

'SET US FREE! SET US FREE!! SET US FREE!!!'

Piers used up the last of the film and tugged at Matt's sleeve. He mouthed *'Let's go'* at him. Keeping low, they moved away.

All the way back, Piers expected they would be discovered. And if they were caught, what then? It was an uncomfortable thought, and he tried to push it to the back of his mind. As they eased themselves through the window they came in by, he noticed that Matt's hands were trembling. When they finally made it to the street Piers was panting with relief himself. Heads down, they set off for the car as fast as they could.

Had either of them looked back, they would have seen the door to the warehouse open.

Rufus came out. Another Companion joined him. They watched Piers and Matt as they turned the corner, then Rufus whispered something to the other bear.

Mr T nodded his head gravely.

'The important thing,' Piers said as they sat in the car outside Matt's house, 'is that you carry on as normal. I know that's going to be difficult, but Rufus mustn't know we suspect anything.'

'Okay, I'll try. But it was incredible, Piers. All that *venom*. Rufus has been behaving badly lately, but I'd never believe...'

'It was a shock, I appreciate that. I just hope they're a bunch of hotheads and it isn't more widespread.'

'And what was all that stuff about, 'Some brothers and sisters beginning to strike for freedom'? What do you think he meant by that?'

'I don't know.' But Piers kept thinking about the photograph he saw at the office and was afraid he did. 'The important thing is that we've got proof.' He held up the camera. 'I'll get these run-off for Baxter. He'll have to listen to me now.'

'And the police?'

'Yes. I'll take copies round to Sergeant Hopkins. With a bit of luck, we can nip this in the bud.'

'I hope you're right, Piers. I really do.'

Piers set about printing the pictures as soon as he got in. Almost all of them came out and they were good. There was Rufus on the ramshackle stage, and shots of his frenzied audience.

Piers realised the photographs didn't prove any kind of evil intent in themselves. But the gathering was probably unusual enough to whet Baxter's curiosity. And the police would want to know what a mob of Companions were doing meeting in a cellar in the middle of the night. It was a breakthrough.

He dropped the prints on the table and yawned. The wall clock showed it was 2am and he thought about getting some sleep.

The phone rang. Wondering who it could be at this hour, he answered it.

'It's Matt, Piers. I had to call you.'

'What's up?'

'Rufus hasn't come home. And Emma wasn't here when I got back.'

'Could she be staying with somebody else?'

'She might be, but she usually tells me if she's going to do that. Thing is, Mandy's not here either.'

'Mandy?'

'Her Companion. I've never known Emma take her out overnight. I looked in Emma's room and it's a shambles. Stuff all over the place, drawers left open. And she's normally very tidy. I'm worried, Piers.'

'Sit tight, I'm coming over.' He hung up.

'I don't think so, Piers.'

He hadn't heard Mr T come in.

'What was that?' Piers tried to sound casual, but that wasn't the way it came out.

'You heard.' Mr T's tone was harsh, his voice level. 'We know you saw us tonight.'

Piers felt a pang of fear. 'Saw you?'

'It's no use pretending.' Mr T was moving toward him. Under other circumstances, his rolling, almost comical gait would have amused Piers. Now it filled him with dread.

He searched desperately for something to say. 'Look, T, I can see that some people have been unkind to Companions –'

The bear threw back his head and gave a short, hollow laugh.

'– and that perhaps I could have been more considerate. But if we work together, we can –'

'No, Piers. It's too late. What you know can harm us, and we've suffered too much to let you ruin things. I'm sorry.' He extended his arm to the radio on the sideboard and snapped it on. Loud music boomed from it.

Then Piers saw the wickedly curved knife in Mr T's other paw.

The sound of the radio smothered his screams.

The bear fed the last of the photographs into the fire in the hearth. He took the poker and jabbed at the burning mass. The dancing flames reflected in his glassy eyes and threw his enormous shadow on the walls and ceiling.

It was a pity about Piers, he thought. As humans went, he wasn't too bad. But it was a matter of survival now, and nobody could be allowed to stand in their way.

Still, he couldn't help remembering better times.

And a big round tear rolled down Mr Thumpy's cheek.

Picking Up The Tab

Adam took another handful of twenty pound notes and threw them into the fire.

They disappeared in a cloud of oily smoke billowing from the old tin bath. He tossed the last of the petrol after them and it ignited with a *whoomp* that made him take an involuntary backward step. Flurries of orange sparks drifted over the lawn. He dipped into the stuffed hold-all for more bundles of money to feed the blaze. Inch-thick wads of fives, tens and fifties turned to brittle ash.

A useless gesture, but Adam felt better for it.

He wiped the back of a hand across his forehead and glanced at the house.

Police sirens wailed in the distance. It wouldn't be long now.

He emptied the rest of the bag into the fire. The wind caught a single fluttering note. Snatching it from the air, Adam crushed the note in his fist and flung it at the inferno.

The sirens were louder.

Frightened as he was, there was no point in running.

Spellbound by the flames, he let the events of the recent past flow through his mind.

It had been just seven days since it began.

A week and a different world ago...

'Do me a *favour*, Wanda!'

'What?'

Adam shoved the compact disc at her. 'You got butter all over it.'

'Oh, yeah. Sorry.'

'Can't you be more careful? I haven't even played it yet.'

'All *right!*' She used her sleeve to wipe off the butter. 'There. That do?' With a jab of her palm the CD slid back across the table to him.

'Thanks,' he said sarcastically. '*Very* thoughtful.'

'If you don't get off my case –'

'Button it, you two.' Their mother slammed down a tray. 'Saturday's one of the few times we have a meal together as a family, and you always ruin it.'

'It's Adam,' Wanda complained, glaring at him, 'looking for something to moan about as usual.'

'Is it my fault I've got a sister with the habits of a pig?'

'*Just once,*' their mother interjected sternly, 'I'd like your father to enjoy his breakfast in peace. Let's have a truce, shall we?'

Wanda scowled and reached for the cereal box. A vigorous shake produced one small cornflake. She looked at the empty packet, then at Adam's overflowing bowl.

The door opened before she could renew hostilities.

'Hi, Dad,' greeted Adam.

'Morning,' Wanda said.

'Uhmm.'

Unshaven, and still in his dressing gown, their dad seated himself. Mum pushed forward a cup of coffee. He took a sip and sliced open a brown envelope from the morning post. The sheet of blue and white paper it contained restored his power of speech. 'Look at this, Babs,' he said, handing the sheet to their mother.

'What is it, Dad?' Wanda asked.

'A telephone bill. A *large* one.'

Adam and Wanda suddenly became very interested in their plates.

'It is a little on the high side,' their Mum agreed.

'More than a little,' Dad grumbled. He eyed his daughter. '*Some* people might consider that the next time they're chattering to their friends.' He turned his attention to his son. 'Or using

36

their computer madam for hours on end.'

'I think you mean *modem*, Dad,' Adam corrected him.

Wanda stifled a giggle.

'Whatever it's *called*, it costs money to operate. Remember that.'

'We're not the only ones living here,' Adam protested.

'You might just as well be! Every time I want to use the 'phone there's either a sniggering teenager or a brainless machine on it.'

Mum stepped in as peacekeeper. 'If you think the amount's unreasonable, Mark, why don't you query it?'

'You know,' he said, folding the bill and putting it in his pocket, 'I might just do that. And while we're on the subject of cutting expenses –'

The doorbell rang.

Adam leapt up, glad of the interruption. 'Okay, that's for me.'

'I'm off, too,' Wanda announced, stuffing a last piece of toast into her mouth and grabbing her coat.

They left their father muttering about them treating the place like a hotel.

The visitor on the doorstep was cleaning his sunglasses with a tissue. He wore a black leather jacket covered with patches. A red sports bag hung from his shoulder.

'Hi, Perry.'

'Morning, Adam.' He grinned. 'Hello, Wanda.'

'How many more times do I have to tell you, Warner?' she bridled. 'It's pronounced *Van*da, not *Won*da. *Van*da, *Van*da... *VAN*-da.'

'As in vandal,' her brother said.

She gave him a menacing look.

'Nah, can't be right,' Perry replied innocently. 'That's like calling me *Var*ner.'

'I don't know why I bother,' she sighed, elbowing aside the smirking pair.

'Bye, *Won*da,' Perry called after her.

'If you keep winding her up like that she's gonna deck you,' Adam laughed.

'I know. But I can't resist it.' Despite the absence of sunlight he put on the shades. 'Let's go.'

In three hours, fourteen minutes and twenty-two seconds, Adam would stand in the shadow of death.

He didn't really like the gaming arcade. The place was seedy, as were some of the people it attracted, so he wasn't sorry when Perry eventually looked at his watch and said he had to leave.

'I've got to be at Cost Savers by one o'clock,' he explained.

'Dressed like *that*?'

He patted the bag. 'Change of gear.'

As they made their way out, Adam said, 'I don't know how you can stand working in that supermarket.'

'It's just until I've saved enough to upgrade my PC, then I'm out of there. My folks say money's a bit tight at the moment.'

'I know all about *that* one,' Adam sympathised.

They emerged blinking into daylight and crowds of weekend shoppers. Perry spotted his bus.

'Call you later!'

'Right.'

Adam decided to head for home.

Death was thirty-one minutes away.

He took the long route, but regretted it when leaden clouds appeared overhead. A raindrop splashed on the back of his hand. A chill wind knifed at him. Flipping up his collar, he walked faster.

Catching a bus for the rest of the journey seemed a good idea. Turning into Terminus Road he walked up the incline leading to the station, where he noticed a man leaning against the waist-high wall of the railway bridge and looking down at the tracks. Nobody else was around.

Seven minutes and fifteen seconds would elapse before

death put in an appearance.

As he drew level with the unmoving figure Adam dug in his pocket for change. Fingers numb with cold, he fumbled the coins and dropped them. They showered tinkling to the pavement.

The man swung around.

Adam was rooted by his terrified expression. Middle-aged and dishevelled, he wore an unkempt blue suit with a slept-in look. He clutched the wall with knuckles as white as his face. His eyes were wild.

The stranger's gaze flicked from Adam to the coins and back again. But he appeared to be more frightened than threatening.

Hoping that was true, Adam bent to pick up the change and said, 'Sorry.'

The man's look of fear softened. He mumbled something.

'Pardon?'

'Money... talks.' His voice was low, hesitant. 'That's what they say, isn't it? Money talks.'

For want of any better response, Adam nodded.

'All it ever said to me was *goodbye*.' The man laughed. It lacked any humour.

Adam smiled politely. A weak smile for a weak joke.

'Now *I'm* saying goodbye to *it*,' the man added. The laugh came again, just as hollow and cynical.

Adam thought he might have been drunk. But his speech wasn't slurred and there was no alcohol on his breath.

Deranged then? Mad, perhaps?

This was getting spooky. And it might just turn nasty. Adam decided it was best to break contact and began moving off.

The man seized his jacket.

'Hey!' Adam tried to twist free.

The man yanked him closer. His eyes blazed. 'The root of all evil,' he rasped. '*Evil.*'

'Yeah, yeah.' Alarmed, Adam made another unsuccessful attempt to pull away.

'They're here. Here, *now*. And they're going to get us.'

'They?'

'They... it... who knows? They've always been here, always collected their dues.'

'Look, I –'

'You tell 'em. Tell everybody!' The man was shaking him. 'Money! Do you hear me? It's pure evil! You've got to *believe* that!'

Adam was near panic, and there was still no one in sight. The man's grip was unbreakable.

A high-pitched whistling noise cut the air.

The man glanced down at the tracks. A train was approaching. He let go of the jacket, Adam apparently forgotten.

As Adam made for the other side of the road, the train's whistle blasted again, louder and keener than before. He looked over his shoulder.

The man was standing on the wall. Arms straight out from his sides, he wobbled unsteadily like a tightrope walker. Metallic vibrations ran through the rails below as the locomotive came closer.

He stared at Adam and bellowed, *The root of all evil!*

Then turned and shuffled to the edge.

Adam opened his mouth to yell but nothing came out. He willed his legs to move but they wouldn't obey.

The racket from the approaching train was deafening. Its whistle screamed once more to add to the din.

And the man stepped off the bridge to keep his appointment with eternity.

Rain pounded against the barred window of the interview room.

Adam was still shaking and had to hold the mug of tea in both hands. The dark, syrupy liquid was too strong and too sweet, but he drank it anyway.

Detective Inspector Frank Ingram sat on the other side of the table going through Adam's statement. A short man with a neatly trimmed moustache, and dressed in an immaculate three-piece suit, Ingram's expression was permanently severe.

He cleared his throat. 'Well, that all seems to be in order. Although what the late Mister Lambert said to you doesn't make a lot of sense.'

'Was that his name?'

'You didn't know?'

'Course not. How could I?'

Ingram laid a brown leather wallet on the table. 'Craig Lambert, according to his ID. He worked for a firm of stockbrokers.'

The Inspector studied Adam's face, as though expecting some kind of reaction.

'All you spoke about was money?' he continued.

'He did most of the talking. A lot of it seemed to be about money, but I didn't really understand what he meant. And, as I said, there was the stuff about somebody being out to get him.'

'He didn't say who?'

'No. He just said 'they'.'

'Hmmm. I see.' He scribbled something in his notepad. 'Is there anything else you'd like to tell me?'

'I don't think so. Except...'

'Go on.'

'I suppose I feel bad about not stopping him.'

Adam thought he saw disappointment on the Inspector's face. 'People who commit suicide are unpredictable. You weren't to know.'

'But *why* did he do it?'

'As far as we can tell he lived a perfectly ordinary life, and there's no record of him trying this before. We may *never* find out why.'

He pushed the statement and a pen across the desk. 'I'd like you to sign this. But before you do, there's something that's been puzzling me.'

'What?'

Ingram glanced at the wallet. 'I mentioned that Lambert had ID on him. But that was all he had. There was no money. No cheque book or credit cards either. Doesn't that strike you as strange?'

'I don't know. Jumping off that bridge was pretty strange.'

'True. Are you *sure* you don't want to add anything to your statement?'

'I'm sure.'

Adam had the uneasy feeling that he was being accused of something.

They sent him home in a police car.

'He was just a poor, disturbed man, Adam. He would have jumped whether you were there or not.'

'I guess you're right, Dad.'

'He is,' Wanda assured him. 'Try to forget about it.'

Adam wanted to believe them, but couldn't shake off the unease that had troubled him for the last twenty-four hours.

They crossed to the High Street. There wasn't much in the way of traffic this early on a Sunday morning, and even less people. The air was cool enough to turn their breath into little huffing clouds of condensation. A sheen of frost covered the pavements.

'I'll get the papers and catch up with you,' Wanda suggested when they reached the newsagents. She held out her gloved hand. Their dad sighed and dropped some change into it. Wanda pushed open the shop's door and went inside.

'The thing is,' Adam said as they resumed their walk, 'I can't stop thinking about that weird conversation I had with Lambert.'

'Don't dwell on it.'

'It's okay; it doesn't upset me or anything. It was sort of fascinating in a funny kind of way. All that stuff about money and evil, and something out to get him. Out to get *all* of us. He looked really terrified, Dad.'

'The man was unwell.' He frowned. 'I'm more concerned about that policeman... What was his name?'

'Detective Inspector Ingram.'

'Yes, Ingram. I don't like him implying you knew something about Lambert not having any money.'

'He didn't actually accuse me of anything. And that *was* a mystery, wasn't it?'

'Well, yes, I can see that,' Father admitted. 'And I suppose if you're a policeman and always dealing with the dark side of human nature you become suspicious of everybody.'

They arrived at the bank and Adam's dad fed his card into the cash dispenser.

'Quiet a minute,' he said, concentrating on punching in his pin number. 'I always have to think about this bit.'

The screen above the keys flashed a red message.

Invalid.

Dad groaned.

'Sure you did it properly?'

'I'm not *that* senile yet, Adam.'

He tried again.

Two more messages appeared, alternating from one to the other.

Unauthorised withdrawal... Inquire at branch... Unauthorised withdrawal...

'*Unauthorised?* What's the matter with it?'

'Let me try.' Adam pressed buttons at random. The message continued flashing.

'Forget it,' his Dad said. 'I'll go to another one.'

A new message came up.

Card withheld... Inquire at branch... Card withheld... Inquire at branch...

'The blasted thing's eaten my card!' He thumped the machine in frustration. 'And what good is it telling us to inquire inside on a Sunday? Now I've got to come back tomorrow and sort this out.'

Wanda came along with a bundle of newspapers under her arm. 'Can I have that fiver you promised me, Dad?'

'*No you can't!* What am I, *made* of money?'

They trudged back in frosty silence.

It was the end of Monday afternoon before Adam got a chance to talk with Perry. As they made their way along the school's bustling corridors, he filled him in on the tragedy. He tried explaining the bizarre things Lambert had said, but Perry was more interested in the gruesome details.

'I bet it was really gross, eh?' he persisted. 'When he went under that train.'

Adam shuddered at the memory. 'What do *you* think, ghoul? It wasn't a movie or an arcade game; this was real.'

'Sorry. It must have been rough.'

'Funnily enough, that isn't what I keep remembering. It's what he *said*. I keep thinking there was some kind of crazy sense in it, you know?'

'No, not really. And if you try to figure it out you'll wind up as mad as he was.'

'Maybe.' He changed the subject. 'Going to Cost Saver?'

'Yeah. Three hour shift.'

'Me and Dad are going there for some shopping. Stick around and we'll give you a lift.'

'Great.'

'Only I've got to see Miss Barrett first, in here.' He indicated the common room door.

Perry leaned against the opposite wall and dropped his bag. 'Okay, I'll wait.'

Adam knocked and went in.

Pamela Barrett was alone. She put down the file she was reading, took off her glasses and smiled.

'Hello, Adam. Take a seat.'

He drew a chair from the large wooden table that dominated the room and sat facing her.

'How are you?' she said.

'Fine.'

Adam had always been comfortable with the young teacher,

maybe because she wasn't *that* much older than him. He could talk to her without feeling patronised the way he did with some of the other members of staff.

She swept aside a stray lock of blonde hair and put the glasses back on. 'The police have been in touch about the... incident at the weekend. It must have been a terrible shock.'

'It wasn't that bad.'

'But after seeing that man –'

'I didn't actually *see* him hit by the train. And I only took a quick peek over the bridge afterwards.'

'How have you been since? Any nightmares, for instance? You can be honest, Adam, there's nothing to be ashamed of.'

'No, it's not affected me that way.'

'You're implying it's affected you in some other way?'

'I keep thinking about what the man, Lambert, said before he jumped. You know he spoke to me?'

'Yes. Want to tell me about it?'

Adam recounted the conversation on the bridge. Miss Barrett made a few notes but didn't interrupt.

When he finished, she said, 'He was ill, Adam.'

'That's what everybody tells me. But suppose he wasn't? Even if he was, why couldn't he have been telling the truth?'

'The truth about *what*? It all sounds very confused to me. He probably *imagined* that somebody was after him. You know, a persecution complex. I expect those references to money were part of his delusions as well. You mustn't get hung-up on what a sick person said to you.'

'Everybody's been telling me that, too. But he seemed... I don't know... genuine. Sincere.'

'Mentally ill people can be very convincing.' She riffled through some papers in the file. 'Would you like me to arrange for you to meet a counsellor, Adam?'

'Thanks, but I don't see the need, Miss Barrett.'

She studied him thoughtfully for a few seconds then said, 'Okay, we'll put the counselling on hold for the time being.'

Adam got up.

'There's, er, something else,' she said.

He noted her uncomfortable expression as he sat down again.

'The policeman in charge of the investigation,' she began flatteringly, 'Detective Inspector Ingram, said he was... puzzled... that Lambert...'

'Didn't have any money on him?' Adam offered.

'Yes. He told you that, of course.' Miss Barrett was practically squirming with embarrassment. 'And, uhm, Mister Ingram wanted me to ask –'

'Whether I stole it?'

'*Adam!* He didn't say that at all.'

'It's what he meant though, isn't it?'

'No. No, of course not. It's just that the people Lambert worked with said he always carried cash and credit cards. The Inspector thought you might have remembered something that –'

'If he suspected me of anything he should have searched me. I wish he had, now.'

'Yes, I suppose he should. Not that I'm saying you –'

'Look, Miss Barrett, I don't know anything about the man not having any money and that's the truth. If he thought money was evil, isn't it logical he wouldn't have any on him?'

'Hmmm, I suppose that would fit in with his psychosis... And I'm afraid the police do tend to see most teenagers in a negative light.' She closed the file. 'Sorry. But I hope you understand that I had to ask.'

'I understand.'

She looked relieved at having got the subject over with. As he was leaving she added, 'I'm here if you need to talk.'

Adam nodded and quietly closed the door behind him.

Perry greeted him with, 'How'd it go?'

'Okay.' His tone didn't encourage further questions.

They walked to the front gate. Adam's father was parked on the other side of the road, impatiently drumming the steering wheel with his fingers.

Once they were underway, Adam said, 'Did you sort out the cash card, Dad?'

'No,' he replied brusquely. 'According to them I'm massively overdrawn on the account.'

'That's not right!'

'I *know* it isn't. Some mix-up with their damned computer, I expect. Or maybe the account's been bloody hacked, I don't know. They're hanging on to the card while they look into things.'

They arrived at the supermarket and cruised the street looking for a parking meter. When they finally found one, Adam's father dug through his pocket for change and pushed coins into the slot.

The meter pinged and displayed the red *penalty* sign.

'I don't *believe* it,' he groaned.

Perry said, 'I really ought to be going, Mister Ferguson.'

'Why don't I go on with Perry and start getting the shopping organised?' Adam suggested.

'Good idea. I'll look for somewhere else to park.'

They left him glaring at the meter.

At the supermarket Perry went off to change while Adam equipped himself with a trolley. But he couldn't concentrate fully for thinking about the odd things that had been happening lately.

Twenty-five minutes later his father turned up, flushed and sour faced.

'What took you so long, Dad?'

'You may well ask. I found another meter and *that* one did exactly the same thing. Soon as I put the coins in it went to penalty.'

'Where's the car then?'

'Had to leave it on a yellow line. So let's not hang around.'

Perry was operating one of the tills. The baggy white coat he wore was several sizes too large and he'd had to roll-up the sleeves.

'They've promised me one that fits,' he said defensively.

Adam tried not to laugh. 'How long have they let you work on the checkout?'

'From this evening. You're my second customer.'

'Can we get on with it, boys?' Adam's father said.

Perry took each item of shopping and ran it across the scanner that automatically registered its cost. The tiny oval screen next to the till displayed the prices in green numerals. All went well until he pressed the total button.

A grinding noise came from the cash register. The screen flickered and showed *00.00*.

Perry looked mystified. 'It's not supposed to do that,' he said, stating the obvious.

He hit the button again.

The screen began flashing a series of random figures.

24.95... 112.16... 92.81... 303.38... 18.42... 77.23... 215.64... 11.09...

With a loud *ting* the cash drawer flew open. The printer clattered and started spewing an endless receipt covered in gibberish.

Other shoppers craned their necks to see what was going on. Beetroot red with embarrassment, Perry jabbed buttons in a futile attempt to control the situation. The ceaseless outpouring of receipt paper continued. Meaningless numbers flashed ever faster on the screen.

The semi-circle of onlookers parted for a stout man identified by a plastic name tag reading *Manager*. His face was as cheerful as an undertaker with a migraine.

'What's going on?' he barked.

'There's something wrong with the till, Mister Harvey,' Perry replied sheepishly.

'I can see *that*. Stand aside.'

He leaned across and punched buttons with a plump finger. It made no difference. Frowning, he reached below the till and wrenched out its plug. The machine instantly died.

Except for the screen, Adam noticed. For a fraction of a second it froze on *666.00* before fading to black.

The manager glared at Perry. 'I think it would be better if you went back to shelf-filling for the time being.'

'It wasn't his fault,' Adam's father said.

The manager gave him a transparently false smile. 'Sorry you've been inconvenienced, sir. If you would care to take your purchases to another –'

'We're in a hurry. Is there any way to speed this up?'

'Of course.' He produced a pocket calculator.

Once the bill was totalled, Adam's dad gave the manager his credit card and he took it away for processing.

When he came back, the synthetic smile had gone.

'It won't be possible to serve you,' he announced.

'*What?*'

'I've just spoken to the credit card company and they say you no longer have a valid account.'

'But –'

'Furthermore, I'm authorised to destroy the card in your presence.'

'Just a minute! What gives you the right –'

'Take it up with the company, Mister Ferguson.'

He slipped a pair of scissors from his pocket and cut the card in two. 'Put those goods back on the shelves, Warner. Good day, sir.'

In a state of shock, father and son left empty-handed. Neither found anything to say to each other, and Adam's insides were gripped by the cold, clammy hand of doubt and apprehension.

When they reached the car there was a parking ticket on its windscreen.

The next morning saw little joy in the Ferguson household.

Adam's mum came in with the post.

'This one's from the telephone company.' She passed Dad a

brown envelope.

He ripped it open and took out two sheets of paper. The first was a letter.

'Is it about the bill you queried?' Wanda asked.

'Yes. Hang on.' He scanned the sheet. 'After the usual guff it says, 'We have reviewed the account and can confirm that the sum requested on your current bill is incorrect'.'

'See?' Mum said with a smile. 'It was worth getting in touch with them.'

'"An amended bill is enclosed",' Dad continued, '"and we take this opportunity of reminding you that payment is due within fourteen days of the receipt of this letter".'

He looked at the second sheet. The colour drained from his face.

'What is it, Mark?' Mum said.

Speechless, he handed her the bill.

'"Total due",' she read, '"eight..."' Her jaw dropped.

'Mum?' Adam prompted, a ripple of icy fear growing in his stomach.

'"Eighteen thousand, two hundred and forty-four pounds, twenty pence".'

Wanda gasped, *What?*'

Dad found his voice. 'I don't know what the *heck's* going on here, but I'm going to get to the bottom of it!' He marched to the telephone and snatched the receiver.

'Don't bother,' Mum told him, 'it's too early.'

He slammed the phone down. 'First the debit card, then the credit card and now this!' His furious gaze turned on the children. 'If you kids have been up to anything with that telephone, I'll –'

'Oh, *come on*, Dad!' Adam retorted indignantly.

'That's nothing to do with us!' Wanda complained.

Mother held up her hand. 'Calm down! All of you. Mark, get on to the telephone people as soon as they open for business. Tell them you want an *itemised* bill right away.'

He grunted, then strode out of the room, slamming the door

behind him.

Adam wondered why he hadn't thought of consulting Cyrus Archer before.

The elderly academic had been his mathematics master for less than a year, but Adam got on with him remarkably well, despite the great difference in their ages. Archer had one of the liveliest intellects Adam had ever encountered, and he thought of him as a kind of mentor. Their friendship had continued beyond his retirement.

Adam yanked the ancient bell-pull, setting off a discordant chime deep in the house's gloomy interior. A few minutes later the door creaked open.

Cadaverously thin, Archer wore his usual faded but once expensive tweed suit, and the thick bifocals that almost seemed a part of him. His unruly hair and goatee beard were a little whiter, but he was otherwise unchanged.

'Adam, how nice to see you; it's been far too long.'

'Evening, Cyrus.' He still felt slightly uncomfortable about Archer's insistence that he use his first name.

Once they settled into a pair of over-stuffed armchairs in the study, the old man came straight to the point. 'Your telephone call was fascinating, and your encounter with the unfortunate Lambert was certainly bizarre. I found what he told you most intriguing.'

Adam was pleased at having someone finally take him seriously. He glanced at the thousands of books surrounding them. 'I thought you'd be interested, knowing your fascination for the more unusual side of human nature.'

'And that I might be able to give you some insight into the workings of a disturbed mind.'

'Well, yes, I suppose so. I've been trying to make sense of it all, and as you're well up on psychology –'

'I believe you've come to the right person,' Archer interrupted, his expression serious, 'but for the wrong reason.' He indicated the overflowing bookshelves. 'The answer may well lie in my other passion.'

'Folklore and myth, you mean? The occult?'

'The word occult merely means "hidden" or "unseen". The great scientist Thomas Alva Edison once said, "We don't know a millionth of one percent about anything," and he was right. But I believe the study of paranormal phenomena could increase that percentage.'

'I don't see the connection with Lambert.'

'Your question is simple, the answer less so, I'm afraid. It's possible that he found out about...'

'About what?'

'I need to think this through, Adam. But it's possible that your experience touches upon a particular area of my research. The key is in that phrase "the root of all evil". The full quotation, of course, is, "The *love* of money is the root of all evil." However, I think the... *intelligence* behind this is far from loveable.'

'You're not making a lot of sense.'

'I know. Be patient.' His face darkened. 'And be careful.'

Adam tried to get him to say more, but he wouldn't be drawn.

'I feel a bit guilty about this, Mum.'

'Don't be silly, Adam. You saved the money and you can do what you like with it. Let's go in.'

The sports shop was filled with lunchtime shoppers. At the footwear section, Adam said, 'Maybe I should leave this for now. I mean, considering the mess we're in –'

'You know we've *got* money, it's just that we can't get to it. Your dad'll sort it out, don't worry.' She took three twenty pounds from her handbag and gave them to him. 'But I'm glad I drew this from the bank last week, before all the trouble with the account.'

'You can say that again.' Adam selected the trainers he wanted.

At the sales desk the cashier held one of the crisp new notes up to the light and frowned. Her expression became harder as she examined the other two.

'Anything wrong?' Adam's mother asked.

'Just a second.' One at a time, the cashier laid the notes on an illuminated platen. Eventually she said, 'I'm afraid these aren't genuine.'

'They *have* to be!'

'I can assure you they're fakes,' the cashier insisted. 'See? No metal strip. And there are other things wrong with them.'

'I don't understand.'

'No, madam,' the woman said coldly. 'Perhaps you better talk to the manager.' She pressed a button beside the till.

'You should be getting back to school,' Adam's Mum told him, her voice dreamy with shock.

'No. I'll stay and –'

'*Don't argue.* There must be some mistake. I'll see what the manager says.'

Once more, Adam experienced the feeling of dread that had visited him regularly in the past few days; the sensation of reality slipping out of gear and turning the world into a hostile place.

Reluctantly, he made his way out of the shop, aware of every eye in the place burning into his back.

When he got home that evening, Adam saw two men come out of his house and drive away in a van.

The atmosphere indoors was tense.

'Who were they?' he asked, hoping it wasn't more bad news.

'Bailiffs,' Wanda said.

'*Bailiffs?*'

'They had a court order,' his Mum explained. Her face was etched with worry. 'It said we owe hundreds of pounds in unpaid parking tickets.'

'*Do* we?'

'Of course not. All we've had this year was the one your

father got outside the supermarket this week. Fortunately we managed to persuade the bailiffs to hold off for a couple of days. Dad's on the phone to the court now.'

'And he isn't happy,' Wanda added darkly.

Adam could see that for himself when his Dad came in from the living room.

'It's like talking to a brick wall!'

Mum laid a hand on his arm. 'Take it easy, Mark, and tell us what happened.'

'I told them it had to be a mistake. *They* said it wasn't. When I pointed out that today was the first we'd heard of it, they obviously didn't believe me.'

'That's crazy.'

'It's on their computer, so it *has* to be right, doesn't it?' he said bitterly. 'I'll have to get a lawyer to deal with this. More expense!'

Unwisely, Wanda said, 'At least you can't blame us this time.'

'We'll have a little less of your lip! Particularly when you're trying to ruin us by sending for that junk!' He waved his hand at a pile of shrink-wrapped magazines on the table.

'I keep telling you, they're nothing to do with me!' she protested.

'What are they?' Adam said.

No one answered so he looked for himself. The dozen or so periodicals were addressed to Wanda. Adam flipped through them and was puzzled by the wide variety of subjects: *Surf-Boarding Monthly, Tropical Fish News, Classic Chess Problems, Golfing World, You and Your Pension...*

Dad brandished a handful of envelopes. 'And these are the invoices for subscriptions to all of them. Nearly three hundred pounds worth!'

'I didn't order them!' Wanda complained. 'Why would I want any of that stuff?'

'Did you get a chance to ring about them today, Babs?' he asked their mother.

'Sorry, Mark, no. I was in the bank most of the afternoon trying to sort out those counterfeit notes.'

'Any luck?'

'Not really. They denied it could have had anything to do with them.'

'Of course.' His voice dripped sarcasm. 'How silly of me to expect something to go right for a change.' He turned to Adam and snapped, 'And why were you so late back from school?'

'Oh. Er, Perry and I dropped into the gaming arcade.'

'You've got money to waste now, have you?'

'No. Actually, I only went to please Perry. He's still a bit ratty about what happened at the supermarket the other day. And... we had a slight problem.'

'What?'

'We got thrown out.' He quickly added, 'We weren't mucking about, honest. It's just that I put some money into one of the machines and it... broke down.'

'Why don't I find that surprising?' his father sighed.

The following day's mail brought another batch of magazines which sparked a further row between Wanda and her father. And the itemised telephone bill, running to eleven pages, contained scores of numbers no one recognised, many with foreign prefixes.

The two remaining letters were worse.

Dad, who looked as though he hadn't slept, gave them the gist of the first one. 'The building society want to know why the mortgage hasn't been paid.'

'But, Mark, it *has*.' Mum said.

'I know.' His anger had been replaced by weariness. He opened the last envelope. 'And this is from my accountant.' He related the contents like someone in a trance. 'The Inland Revenue have found a discrepancy in my tax returns. They're demanding immediate payment of...'

'Yes?'

'Twenty thousand, near enough.'

Mum gasped.

'That's not all. There's a problem with VAT, too. They want what the accountant calls a "substantial" sum. He finishes by saying, "I must remind you that as a self-employed person it is your responsibility to conduct your financial affairs in an open and honest manner." And here's the kicker. "It is my duty to inform you that failure to do so could result in a large fine or even imprisonment."'

A knot of fear tightened in Adam's chest.

'You're not going to jail are you, Dad?' Wanda exclaimed.

'Course not, dear,' mother told her. 'We're just having some bad luck at the moment. It can't last forever.'

'Can't it?' Dad said.

The telephone rang and mother answered it. 'Adam, it's Cyrus Archer. Why don't you take it in the other room?'

When he got to the extension, Adam told the professor it wasn't the best time for a chat.

'I understand. And in fact it would be unwise for us to speak too freely on the telephone.'

Adam was puzzled by that, but let it pass.

'Could you come and see me tomorrow evening?' his old teacher said. 'It's very important.'

'We've some family problems at the moment, but I think so.'

'Are they of a financial nature?'

'How did you know?'

'I won't go into that now. But please be here tomorrow. It's *vital.*'

Adam promised he would and hung up.

He spent the rest of the evening trying to rid himself of the thought that things were getting out of control.

At school, Perry greeted him with surprising news.

'Heard about Pamela Barrett?'

'No, what?'

'She's only won a bundle on a lottery ticket.'

'Yeah? How much?'

'Two hundred and fifty grand! And they say she's never bought a ticket before. Talk about luck, eh?'

'Wow. I wonder what she'll do with it.'

'Gonna travel the world, apparently.'

'I'll have to congratulate her.'

'You're too late. She's quit already. Came in early this morning, cleared her desk and left.'

'That was a bit sudden, wasn't it?'

Perry shrugged. 'Perhaps she likes acting on impulse.'

Adam couldn't understand why he felt there was something unsettling about Miss Barrett's good fortune.

A storm was brewing.

Lightning flashed, briefly illuminating the shadowy recesses of Cyrus Archer's study. Distant thunder rolled.

As Adam finished relating his family's troubles the old man snapped on a table lamp. A pool of soft orange light embraced them, intensifying the surrounding gloom.

'I'm having some financial difficulty myself at present,' Archer said.

'Really?' The nameless dread crept back.

'Yes. My private pension, usually paid into my bank like clockwork, has gone astray. It looks as though they're beginning to take an interest in me too. I'm surprised it took so long.'

'I don't understand any of this.'

'I shall endeavour to explain. But you may regard what I say as the ramblings of a deranged wrinkly.'

Adam smiled. 'I doubt that.'

'Very well.' Archer paused for a moment to gather his thoughts. 'What would you say if I told you we have always unknowingly shared this world with another life form at least as intelligent as us? And I'm not talking about dolphins.'

'I'd say tell me more.'

'Then bear with me. Human history is littered with

references to this... *species*. In Biblical times, people believed in demons. And angels, of course. The Middle Ages abounds with tales of vampires and werewolves. Sea serpents were reported as early as the second century, although sightings are much less common now. Ghosts and spirits seem always to have been with us, and the nineteenth century saw the first recorded instances of poltergeists. Our own century has the Yeti and the Loch Ness monster, not to mention UFOs and their presumed alien occupants.'

'I don't know where this is leading, Prof. But I'd be more convinced if anyone had ever caught one of these things.'

'Suppose that's because they only take physical form when it suits them? Imagine an intelligence composed of pure thought that can become whatever it chooses.'

'So all these different supernatural creatures and so on are –'

'A single, controlling intelligence that takes many guises. And don't you see, Adam? It adopts a new form for each age.'

'Why?'

'To suit changing human beliefs. There can't be many people these days who take vampires or fairies seriously, but you'll find plenty of folk who accept the existence of, say, flying saucers.'

'But what's the point of it? Why would this intelligence behave that way?'

'Because it's in its nature to sow discord, confusion... and fear.'

Lightning flooded the room and thunder boomed.

'Oh, yes,' Archer continued, 'there's a great deal of evidence indicating this thing is malevolent. The *real* history of the human race is of an unending war between the powers of Darkness and Light. We live side by side with an invisible empire. An empire of evil.'

'I still don't see how this all ties in with me and my family.'

'*Think*, Adam. This life form is jealous of us; it resents our dominance of the planet. It may even be older than our race; it could have been here when our primitive ancestors heaved themselves from the swamp. Up to now, its battle with us has been a draw. But given its ability to assume any guise, and its ambition to replace us, what form do you think it might take *now?*'

'Monsters of some sort? Or –'

'There's no need! Our civilisation has produced something that gives it the opportunity to finally conquer us.'

'I don't see what that could be.'

The financial system!'

'You can't be serious.'

'It sounds insane, I know. But can you think of a more powerful force in the world today than money? Look how it rules our lives. You've seen yourself how difficult things get when the system breaks down. *Becoming* that system is the perfect way to manipulate and ultimately destroy us!'

'Why hasn't anybody realised this before?'

'I believe they have. But the life form guards itself jealously. It doesn't take any risks. Lambert, for example, who must have discovered the truth somehow, was driven to suicide.'

'But how did he find out?'

'Perhaps by chance, like you. It hardly matters now.'

Adam paled. 'And he spoke to me before he killed himself.'

'Exactly. You *know*. That's why you're being persecuted. This thing will get at you any way it can. Where it can't do so directly, it applies pressure to your family and friends. It has many weapons at its disposal. Take Pamela Barrett. There's a possibility she might have tried to help you, so she was, in effect, bribed to go away.'

'What does this intelligence expect me to do?'

'I don't think it expects you to do anything. I think it wants to eliminate you.'

'Just a minute, Cyrus. Don't take this the wrong way, but I'm far from buying your theory. Why try to get rid of me if I don't believe in it?'

'As I said, this entity doesn't take any chances. If there's just a possibility of you believing, or passing on your story to someone who would, that's enough to have you... *silenced.*'

Adam thought how sad it was that the professor had allowed his imagination to run away with him. Maybe he was turning senile.

He didn't tell his parents what Cyrus Archer said. They had enough to worry about.

The next morning, Saturday, they both went out early to see the accountant.

Mid-morning, the post arrived, and there was a package for Adam. It contained a note and a key.

The note read -

Dear Adam,
I am sending this in advance of our meeting tonight. If anything
happens to me before then, use the key to let yourself into my house.
You will find a letter addressed to you in the top drawer of my desk. It
will tell you what I would have explained this evening. Should anything
happen to me after our meeting, you will understand why. In that
event, my library may provide a clue to defeating them. I have good
reason to believe we are in danger. Take care.
C.A.

It made him realise how seriously the professor took his theory. Surely there couldn't have been any truth in his fanciful story?

Could there?

The doorbell broke Adam's reverie.

He heard Wanda answer it, and the clump of boots overlaid with unfamiliar voices in the hall. Adam stuffed the key into his pocket.

Detective Inspector Ingram came into the kitchen. Two uniformed officers stood behind him.

There were no pleasantries. 'I need to talk to you,' the policeman said. 'I understand you're acquainted with a Mister

Cyrus Archer.'

'What about it?'

'He's been seriously injured.'

'*No!* What happened?'

'There was a raid on a betting shop in Union Street. He got in their way outside and was shot.'

'Shot?' Adam thought of the note. 'Where *is* he? I have to go and –'

'I'm afraid not. He's in intensive care. And I'm only telling you because we found your name in his address book.'

'Mine couldn't have been the only name in it. Why come to me?'

'I'm mentioning this because it seemed quite a coincidence as we were coming here anyway.'

Adam was baffled. 'Why?'

'In connection with another of your friends. Perry Warner.'

Wanda appeared at the doorway. 'Is Perry okay?'

'He's under arrest on suspicion of stealing money from the supermarket where he works part-time.'

'Never!' Adam said. 'Perry's the most honest –'

'And we have reason to believe,' the inspector interrupted, 'that he had an accomplice.'

Adam could see where this was going. 'You mean *me?*'

'We understand you and your father tried to obtain goods under false pretences there the other day.'

'It wasn't like that. We –'

'And there's a report of you and your *mother* attempting to pass counterfeit notes in a sports shop.'

'But –'

'Add to that the little mystery of Craig Lambert's missing money and it begins to look like we're dealing with a criminal family here. I'm going to have to ask you to come down to the station.'

Wanda said, 'This is ridiculous!'

'Stay out of it, young lady,' Ingram warned.

'You're not taking my brother!' Without warning, she flung herself at the inspector. The other two policemen moved in and struggled with her. 'Run, Adam!' Wanda shouted. *Run!*

He hesitated for a second, unwilling to leave her.

Then fled through the back door.

Adam went to Cyrus Archer's house.

When he looked in the desk for the letter he found a hold-all crammed with bank notes. He knew it didn't belong to Archer. It was there to implicate him in something, to frame and discredit him.

Adam was a believer now. For all the good that did him.

And he knew real fear.

The least he could do for his elderly friend was get rid of the contents of the bag. He found an old galvanised bath and a can of petrol in the garden shed.

They made a perfect... *funeral pyre.*

The shrieking police cars drew up as he gave the last of the notes to the flames. He didn't bother to run. Where would he go? He was up against something ruthless and all-pervading. And as Archer said, it took no chances. It had isolated him, and left him with a story no one would believe.

'Destroying evidence, are we?'

He turned. Detective Inspector Ingram was walking toward him across the lawn.

Adam had no doubt that more 'evidence' would be produced. It even occurred to him to wonder how much it took to bribe a policeman. Anything was possible.

Ingram took him by the arm. 'Running away like that wasn't very smart. It makes you look guilty of something. What's the matter, cat got your tongue?'

'I don't think anything I say is going to make much difference somehow.'

The inspector smiled. It wasn't pleasant.

'You can put money on it,' he said.

SPOIL

And ye shall know the truth. And the truth shall set you free.
— Gospel of St John

At precisely 3.15 pm Cardinal Paolo Fabrizzi kept his appointment to kill the Pope.

Vatican protocol required he be escorted to the pontiff's chambers. The aide carrying out this task wore the usual air of stiff formality, yet Fabrizzi was aware of envious, sidelong glances from the man. Given the vivid scabs covering the Cardinal's face this was hardly surprising, and as they walked he used a corner of his lace handkerchief to dab at a trickle of yellow pus weeping from one of them.

In the welcoming cool of the private meditation room, His Holiness the Bishop of Rome rose from prayer and embraced his assassin. They crossed to a sofa facing a low table laid with an exquisite bone china tea set, and sat together in silence until the aide discreetly exited.

'It ill suits to ask if you are well, Paola.' The Pope's tone betrayed a weariness belying his years.

'I am well enough, Holy Father.'

'And you are prepared for your... undertaking?'

'With the help and guidance of the Almighty, yes, Holy Father.'

God's Shepherd sighed. 'At least He has not forsaken *you*, old friend.'

'Your Holiness, I...'

The response was waved aside. 'This is not bitterness, Paola.

Certainly I feel none towards you. I have examined my conscience, and while at a loss to understand how I have failed our Lord, I know Him to be just.' He smiled weakly. 'Since our days in the seminary I have devoted myself to a life of piety. Apparently that has not been enough. But whatever error I may have committed I will not compound it with the ultimate affront. That would surely condemn my immortal soul.'

'Have all avenues been explored, Father? After all, who are we to interpret the will of God?'

'You clutch at straws.' He toyed with the crucifix at his chest, regretting the tetchiness of his response. 'I do not presume to know God's purpose, Paolo, but I cannot believe He would wish the true faith harmed because of the failings of His servant. You act for the good of the Church, do not trouble yourself on that score. Your salvation is doubly assured.'

'And you?'

'I commend myself to His infinite mercy.'

Fabrizzi moved to kneel before the Pope, taking his hand and kissing it. 'Forgive me for what I must do, Holy Father.' He stifled a watery cough and swallowed. 'Give me your blessing.'

The Vicar of Christ glanced at the sores speckling the Cardinal's bald pate and steeled himself against thoughts of jealousy. 'Under the circumstances,' he said, 'I may not be the most appropriate person to do that.'

'*Envy!*' the Reverend Mason Dexter yelled, punching the air. The crowd echoed him with a roar. Six more times he led, and they answered, each return louder than before.

'PRIDE! COVETOUSNESS! LUST! GLUTTONY! ANGER! SLOTH!'

The stadium, filled to capacity, rocked with applause, shouts and whoops as the litany was completed. A tiny figure standing on the edge of the podium, his image enlarged to gigantic proportions by three massive telecast screens high above, Dexter raised his arms for silence.

'Mortal sins, brothers and sisters! *Mortal sins!*'

A rumble of agreement swept the mass.

'Who can say they have not transgressed in the eyes of the Lord? But now – now, brethren – our store of past wrongs is about to be weighed against us!'

Hallelujahs rang out as one of the cameras zoomed in on the rangy Texan. For a fraction of a second the screens blurred, then refocused and filled with a close-up of Dexter's sweat-sheened face, the angry scarlet weals strangely incongruous under his neatly coiffured silver grey hair.

'For all things there is a season, brothers and sisters! A time to keep and a time to cast away! A time to be born... and a time to die!'

A chorus of amens.

At the back of the podium an organ struck up *Nearer My God to Thee* as two lines of people of varying ages began to file on stage, women and children from the left, men from the right. Some rode wheelchairs or shuffled on crutches. Each was accompanied by a young male or female attendant, dressed identically in dark blue blazers, with white trousers for the men, pleated white skirts for the women. Unlike any of their charges, about half had their faces and in some cases hands, peppered with sores.

'I carry my burden happily,' Dexter continued, 'and thank God for my tribulations! For the cross I bear assures my everlasting reward! And I want to share that blissful burden with every one of you here tonight!'

The crowd thundered its approval.

A girl of about eight, steered by a smiling helper, arrived at his side. Dexter pointed the microphone at her.

'What's your name, honey?'

The child, red-faced, studied her feet. 'Amy,' she mumbled.

'And do you believe in the everlasting grace of our Lord Jesus Christ, Amy?'

Staring up at him wide-eyed, right thumb seeking the

comfort of her mouth, she could only nod. Dexter passed the mike to an attendant, relying on the cordless pinned to his lapel, and placed a hand on each of her temples. He brought his face close to hers and she blinked rapidly, seemed on the verge of tears.

'No need to be frightened, darling.' On his knees now, still cradling her, he threw back his head and addressed a point on the distant ceiling.

'Oh Lord, whose compassion passeth all understanding, look kindly upon this child, that she may bask in the radiance of Your love for all eternity! With the laying-on of hands I pray that the gift You have seen fit to bless me with will pass to her! Allow this innocent to join the band of the select and let her deliverance be assured! Thank You, Lord! Amen!'

The girl looked bewildered and took an uncertain step back as Dexter stood again. A ripple of applause and more hallelujahs broke out as she was led away.

Reverend Dexter's attention passed to the next in line, an overweight middle-aged man, who seemed even more perplexed than the child. A nervous tic spasmed the corner of his mouth as the evangelist laid a hand on his shoulder.

'Repeat after me, brother. I abhor and reject the Devil and all his...'

Sheila Harvey killed the picture and tossed the remote aside. Reaching for the mirror again, she studied herself. She pulled and stretched the skin on her cheeks, examined the whites of her eyes, checked her tongue.

Nothing.

For at least the tenth time that day she pushed away the increasingly familiar mixture of relief and disappointment. Determined to concentrate on the job at hand, she turned back to the laptop's screen and re-read what she had written.

Dr Preston Geddes of the Institute for Genetic Research today called on the government to make more funds available for the study of SPOIL.

Dr Geddes adds his voice to many in the scientific community who maintain research is being hampered by lack of finance. Expressing alarm at the speed with which the disease is spreading, and the failure to make any significant progress in understanding its nature or origin, Dr Geddes also hinted that pressure groups may be influencing government policy.

'Its peculiarly selective character, unparalleled in the history of epidemiology, makes SPOIL a particularly tough nut to crack,' he said. 'Since the first reported case, some eight months ago, there has not been one documented instance of any infected person surviving. That should be of grave concern to the authorities.'

He added that all attempts to arrest or even postpone the advance of the disease had failed. "The prognosis never varies. The thing gets a hold and runs its course irrespective of our efforts. There is no apparent vector. Indeed, transmission remains as much of a mystery now as when we first became aware of the condition."

What significance did he see in the fact that so far the only factor that seemed to link the victims was ...

She was holding a cigarette and didn't even remember lighting it. Stubbing it out, she consulted her notes. What *was* the common factor? Or, rather, how to put it? She bent to the keyboard.

... social rather than medical? Social wasn't quite the right word, but would do for now. She carried on typing. *"As a scientist," Dr Geddes responded, "I find that aspect both fascinating and an affront to logic. There must be another element the infected share which we simply haven't discovered yet."*

He was less forthcoming on allegations that powerful lobbies are frustrating the medical profession's ability to combat the disease. Choosing his words with care, Dr Geddes would only comment that, "Certain groups purporting to act in the best interests of the people they represent may be placing obstacles in the way of research. Encouraging their followers to refuse treatment, as they have in some cases, is an act of gross irresponsibility."

He added, "The unique properties of SPOIL, and the extraordinary way it manifests in its terminal stage, presents us all with a tremendous challenge. Potentially, SPOIL makes AIDS pale into insignificance. It is a major risk to an as yet unknown percentage of the global population."

An unknown percentage of the population. That, Sheila thought, was the point. We think we know who is most at risk, but the evidence makes no sense. And how do you fight a disease people want to catch?

Once more, she stretched for the mirror.

In the slums of Delhi she was known simply as Little Mother. Diminutive in stature she certainly was, but her calling had precluded Sister Kathleen from achieving the status of true motherhood. To the starving and dispossessed to whom she devoted her life, however, Little Mother was an object of reverence.

She was vomiting into an orange plastic bucket.

Doctor Miller handed her a Kleenex. She wiped her mouth and dropped the soiled tissue into a bin, then allowed him to take her arm as they returned to his desk. They seated themselves, and without preamble the doctor delivered his verdict.

'Insofar as I can be sure, your suspicions are confirmed. You have SPOIL.'

Contradictory emotions flooded her. Joy mingled with concern for the two hundred and eleven souls she currently ministered to. What would become of them? Would many follow her?

'How long?'

'If it takes its usual path, and we have no reason to believe otherwise, six to eight weeks.'

Kathleen closed her eyes. The heat, which she had learned to tolerate years before, suddenly returned with an oppressiveness she recalled from her early days in India. The ceaseless racket from the street outside, also long ignored, washed over her.

'Sister?'

She found herself back in the doctor's makeshift surgery, the hub of her mission. 'I am sorry, Edward. I was thinking that there is much to do and so little time. We have seen few cases here so far. What can I expect?'

'The nausea you are experiencing marks the onset. It will pass in a few days. You will begin to develop sores, accompanied by occasional headaches and sporadic rigidity in your limbs. There may well be a constriction of your vocal chords. You are aware of how it ends, of course.' He paused. 'There is nothing I can do to alleviate any of these symptoms.'

'Nor would I want you to.'

'Naturally.'

A realisation struck her. 'Oh dear, Edward. Please forgive my selfishness. I am so preoccupied with my own position I was forgetting that you –'

He raised his hand. 'No matter. We all await God's judgment now, and I trust to His wisdom. There is time for me yet.'

She made to leave. 'I will be in the chapel giving thanks, should I be needed. I will pray for your deliverance.'

Her martyrdom, he knew, was just a matter of time. But there would be many martyrs, and who would be left to revere them?

'Sister Kathleen.'

At the door, she stopped and turned to him. 'Yes?'

'Congratulations.'

They smiled.

'Forgive me, Father, for I have...'

'I think we can drop the formalities, Bernard.' Father O'Halloran shifted uneasily in his half of the confession booth. 'Did you bring it?'

'I have it here, Father.'

'Keep your voice down, man!'

The priest slid closer to the grill separating them. 'Are you absolutely sure it's the... genuine article?' The rasping whisper only emphasised his edginess.

'I am, Father.'

'And where did it...'

'Be assured that the source, shall we say, met the

requirements.'

Father O'Halloran shuddered. He relegated thoughts of "the source", and how he or she may have been persuaded to cooperate, to the back of his mind. Best stick to the business at hand.

'Pass it to me as we leave the confessional, but be sure no one sees us.'

'As you say, Father. And you have the, er, wherewithal?'

'Yes.'

'It's only to cover my expenses, as I explained, Father.'

'Yes, I understand, Bernard. Let's get this over with.'

They emerged from the booths to find only two other people in the church, a pair of elderly women sitting to the left of the altar, engrossed in whispered conversation. Neither paid them any attention.

Bernard dragged a small package, a sticky-taped newspaper bulk, from his overcoat pocket. The priest produced a thick brown envelope. Following a surreptitious glance in the direction of the old ladies, they were exchanged.

'You know what you have to do, Father?'

'Yes, yes. Good day to you.' He hurried off.

Locking the study door behind him he swept away the debris that littered his desk and tore at the parcel. A small glass vial of darkly red liquid, a plastic hypodermic and a shrink-wrapped needle tumbled out. Father O'Halloran sank into a chair and rolled up his sleeve.

Outside, Bernard Harris finished counting the notes and slipped them into his trouser pocket. Probably from the parishioners anyway, he thought. Plenty of that flowing in these days. People trying to buy their way into paradise, the hypocrites. Like the old fool back there.

Easing himself into his car, he looked over at the church. St Helen's, was it? You had to laugh. St Jude, patron saint of hopeless cases, would be more to the point.

He turned the ignition and engaged gear. Obviously the

priest was too stupid to know you couldn't deliberately catch SPOIL. Bernard could attest to that aspect of the disease personally.

The thought of Father O'Halloran trying to curry favour with God by injecting pig's blood brought a bitter grin as he gunned the engine and took off down the street.

After four hours of reverse healing Dexter was exhausted.

There were more and more of them every night, seeking an intermediary with the Creator, a conduit to redemption.

It was sweet. Dexter took the credit for those who got SPOIL, publicly paraded them and encouraged others to come forward. As for those who didn't catch it – well, they only had themselves to blame. Or God. In any event chance was on his side. Some were bound to develop the disease, the law of averages saw to that.

But none of this relieved his apprehension.

He acknowledged the audience's ear-splitting farewell with a wave, and as he left the stage ushers were starting to pass along the aisles, many of their donation pails already brimming.

To get to his dressing room he had to pass through the area where tonight's meeting was being relayed nationwide via satellite. He reciprocated a nod from the linkman who was cueing in SALVATION TV's next offering with a voice-over.

'That's all from the Reverend Mason Dexter's ministry for tonight, folks. And remember, pledges can be phoned in on any of our toll-free numbers. In a few minutes you can see another edition of Bell, Book and Buzzer, the fastest-moving religious quiz show with the biggest prizes! But first, more zany, uplifting adventures featuring that lovable cartoon character Magnificat!'

Dexter slammed the door behind him and was met by a personal assistant waving her clipboard. 'One hundred and forty-two thousand last night,' she intoned, crisply, 'getting on for three times that amount promised. It's up again.'

'Thanks, Rebecca. Send June in here right away, would you?

And see we're not disturbed.'

Shortly, June Bridges, carrying a small valise, entered without knocking. It was the sort of privilege allowed only to the most trusted of his inner circle.

'Lock it.'

She secured the door, then joined him in front of the mirror, flipping the switch to the neon strip above it.

'Seems like a good take again tonight.'

'Yeah.' He looked preoccupied.

'And?'

'And I don't know how much longer I can get away with it.'

'You should worry, Dex. The way the money's rolling in we can —'

'Do you know what those people would do if they found out?' He inclined his head in the direction of the muted clamour from outside. 'They'd tear me to pieces.'

'What's really eating you?'

'Never could keep anything from you, June. I keep wondering why I've been passed over.'

'You're starting to believe it!'

'Aren't you?'

She ignored the question, countered with one of her own. 'So it really bugs you, does it? Not having SPOIL, I mean.'

He caught her eye in the mirror. 'Suppose everything they say about this plague is true?'

'Dex...'

'No, listen. I've seen it. I've seen the way it is at the end, when it takes them. It's not... natural, June. There's no disease ever known could do that to a person.'

'They'll sort it out, find some kind of cure. Meanwhile we clean up.'

'You can't think that. Not now.'

Tight-lipped, she hefted the case, slamming it on the dressing table. 'We should get you seen to.'

He knew her well enough to realise there was no point

arguing, even though he suspected she was just as troubled. Anyway, what was the use? Events were overtaking them all, and he had never felt less in control of his life.

'All right.' He expelled a breath. 'It was real hot out there tonight. You're going to have to fix it stronger next time.' With thumb and index finger he took hold of a scab above his upper lip and pulled. The latex elongated and snapped like a piece of old chewing gum. 'Get this shit off me.'

'Good evening. I'm John Whitestone and this is Forum, your weekly guide to current affairs.'

As the opening music swelled the camera pulled back to take in his guests, occupying a semicircle of swivel chairs, then cut back to him.

'Tonight we address what may be the most important crisis facing the world in living memory, a crisis many contend is the profoundest humanity has *ever* faced. According to the World Health Organisation, Spontaneous Poly-Organic Idiopathic Lupus Erythematosus, commonly known as SPOIL, is now officially designated a pandemic. Estimates of the number of fatalities resulting from the disease vary, but are conservatively put at fifteen million. At least twenty times that number are said to have contracted it. Catching SPOIL means dying. There is not a single case of anyone recovering from it. More remarkable even than the figures are the nature of its victims and the manner of their passing. It's these aspects we shall be discussing here. I'm joined by Archbishop Alan Beaumont, himself a SPOIL sufferer; The Times' medical correspondent, Sheila Harvey, and Gerald Sterling, Chairman of the Rationalist Alliance. If we can turn to you first, Archbishop. You were diagnosed as having SPOIL several weeks ago. Tell me...'

Sheila Harvey hoped Whitestone would manage to avoid saying it.

'... how did you feel?'

He didn't, and she squirmed inwardly at the cliché.

73

The Archbishop, just beginning to display the characteristic facial eruptions, seemed oblivious to Whitestone's crassness. 'Well, John, certainly not like a sufferer, as you stated in your introduction. In common with believers world-wide, I accept that SPOIL is a benediction, the culmination of God's plan.'

'You have no doubt about that?'

'None whatsoever.'

'I'll come back to you in a moment, Archbishop, but I'd like to bring in Sheila Harvey here. Miss Harvey, you have written extensively on SPOIL. What conclusions have you reached?'

She suppressed a smile. 'That's a big question, bearing in mind some of the finest scientific intellects admit to being baffled by it. But what Archbishop Beaumont had to say sums up what must be the majority view.'

'The majority view,' Whitestone interjected, 'but not the only view. Are you saying you subscribe to it?'

'The honest answer would be that I don't know. However, it should now be apparent to the most sceptical observer that SPOIL represents something more than just a public health risk.'

'We were talking before going on air and you mentioned that you had a fairly traditional religious upbringing.'

Sheila resented the breach of confidence but resolved not to show it. She merely nodded in agreement.

'I understand you were brought up in a convent, in fact, and subsequently moved away from religion. So your feelings about the present situation are presumably mixed?'

'I have, let's say, reservations about organised religion. But it was the Church I rejected, not necessarily my belief.'

'Do you regret that decision now?'

'No. It seems to me that what you're implying is based on a misconception about SPOIL. Membership of a church, sect or cult isn't in itself any kind of guarantee. It seems to go much deeper than that, to the core of faith. All those people rushing to join up, if I can put it that way, miss the point.'

Whitestone turned from her. 'Of course it's not only the

churches that are seeing their attendances swell, is it, Gerald Sterling? There's been a large increase in the ranks of the non-believers too, hasn't there?'

'There has. Many people who see SPOIL as a purely medical problem resent the religious establishment hijacking it for their own purposes. But, to be honest, we've had nearly as many deflections as new recruits.'

'Yes,' the Archbishop put in, 'this must present you with a dilemma. I am satisfied that SPOIL is divinely inspired. When you too come to this realisation, as you must, your position will be untenable.'

'Perhaps,' Sterling responded. 'I think it represents more of a quandary for other groups. For the sake of argument let's accept that SPOIL exclusively afflicts the religious. How do you define religious? There are cases of atheists and agnostics dying from it. Do we assume they were secret believers? Muslims seem widely affected, but what about Hindus, Taoists, Sufis and the various cultists? Individuals in all these groups have gone down with it, even if the groups themselves, en masse, don't seem to.'

'I've given that some thought,' Sheila said. 'Statistics are a mess at the moment because nobody can deal with the sheer volume, but I've yet to come across more than a handful of cases involving Buddhists or Rastafarians, for example. So perhaps the atheists you mentioned really were closet believers, even if they didn't acknowledge it to themselves.'

'What do we think this means?' Whitestone asked.

'Maybe that the factor uniting the victim is not religious belief alone,' Sheila replied 'but, specifically, belief in a monotheistic deity.

'"You shall have no other gods before me."' The Archbishop's quote silenced them all until Gerald Sterling broke the impasse.

'That's going to make life a bit uncomfortable for Satanists.'

'I beg your pardon?' The clergyman looked puzzled.

'Well, when you think about it, Satan-worshippers must by

definition be believers in God. They can hardly accept one without the other, can they? It might be interesting to see how *they're* faring with SPOIL. Anyway, this is all academic until someone proves SPOIL really is God-given. Needless to say, I use the word God advisedly.'

'Quite.' Whitestone could see the discussion slipping out of his control. 'I think what we're saying is that there are no pat answers.'

Just pat statements, Sheila reflected.

'But it is the final stages of SPOIL,' their host went on, direct to the camera, 'that presents the biggest challenge to believers and non-believers alike. And, despite the high number of deaths, thus far comparatively few of us have witnessed that terminal stage. Death, except in exceptional circumstances, is an intensely private occurrence. All the more so with SPOIL because of the religious connotations so many people attach to it. At this point we want to run a piece of film Forum has obtained showing the final moments of a SPOIL victim. We believe this is the first time such scenes have been shown on British television, and would like to stress that we do it with the consent of the family concerned. What you are about to see was shot by an amateur cameraman, so the quality may not be up to our usual standard. It was filmed in a small hospice in a suburb of Peru. Viewers are advised that they may find it disturbing.'

Sheila wasn't expecting this. No one had said anything about it, and from the expression on Gerald Sterling's face he was equally surprised. The Archbishop seemed unmoved, however, and she guessed he had been forewarned. At least they had had that much sensitivity.

The monitor beside them began its five-four-three-two-one lead-in.

It had all the hallmarks of being filmed with a hand-held camcorder or possibly a mobile. A man, probably in his mid-forties, eyes closed, lay propped up against pillows in a hospital bed. Every inch of his exposed flesh was scabrous. Mostly out of shot someone sat to his right. As the camera approached, the man in the bed opened his eyes, something like a smile lighting his face. The picture swayed and briefly showed the person sitting by him. A grey-haired woman, in her late sixties perhaps. His mother? She was twisting a rosary in her hands. The camera moved back to the man and steadied. He seemed to be trying to rise.

Sheila sneaked a look at the others. Beaumont was completely still, entranced by the flickering screen. Sterling, beyond him, sat with his mouth hanging open. In other circumstances she would have laughed.

She turned her attention back to the screen in time to see the final act. Even softened by the medium of film she found it too intense, and during the last seconds she had to look away. They all did.

Oh God, she thought. *Oh God.*

Veronica Flint speculated on the unreliability of au pairs. Maria, the current one, was proving no better than any of her predecessors; only interested in boyfriends, wanting to go out all the time, forever bringing unsuitable people to the house... Now the wretched girl had been half an hour behind with supper and had made Veronica late for the public meeting at St Helen's.

As a leading light in the burgeoning Morality Now movement, Mrs Flint felt it beholden upon her to set an example, and lax punctuality went against the grain. She put her foot down and the speedometer nudged sixty.

It was bad enough having to wait with such patience for God to give her SPOIL. She had no fear He would not, of course, but wished He would hurry up and get around to her. Needing to worry about feckless, lazy – and doubtless promiscuous – little madams taking advantage of her generosity was an additional millstone she could well do without, thank you very much.

Heaven knew it wasn't as though Mrs Flint was

unreasonable in what she asked the girl to do. Looking after the children, doing the housework, shopping, running errands, some light chores in the garden, washing the car, a little redecorating; nothing a young woman should find too taxing. All this talk about hearing someone in her family back in Argentina, or wherever it was, had SPOIL was just a way of getting at her employers, Mrs Flint was sure of that. Well, she would have to go, that's all there was to it.

She selected a middle-of-the-road music station on the car radio, and had barely begun to relax into its soothing string versions of popular classics when a strident voice replaced them.

'We interrupt this programme to bring you a newsflash. The Vatican has just announced that His Holiness the Pope has passed away as a result of contracting SPOIL.'

Trust the Catholics to get in first, Mrs Flint thought.

'Rumours that His Holiness had been suffering from the disease, fuelled by his recent absence from the public eye, have been circulating for several months. In a brief statement, the Vatican referred to the Pope's significant contribution to world harmony, and his much-publicised initiative to bring the Catholic Church to a closer understanding with other major Christian denominations.'

God obviously wanted to put a stop to *that*, she felt sure.

'His Holiness has been taken by the Almighty to sit at His right hand,' a spokesman said. 'In keeping with the traditions and law governing these matters, the pontiff's final moments were witnessed by his personal physicians and a triumvirate of senior officials of the true church, who bore witness to the dignity of his passing. All followers of the faith are urged to pray for the deliverance of his immortal soul.

'One of those thought to have been present was Cardinal Paolo Fabrizzi, a lifelong friend and colleague of the Pope, who is known to have SPOIL himself.

'As Catholics fill St Peter's Square to overflowing tonight, speculation turns to the question of the Pope's successor. Many of the cardinals who will make the choice are already in Rome, and their decision will be taken against a background unprecedented in the Vatican's history. In light of SPOIL, the

question being asked is...'

Bernard Harris, having stopped off at a pub to down seven or eight large whiskies with Father O'Halloran's money, was resuming his journey homeward sans seat belt.

He had no recollection of turning on the radio, but the announcement of the Pope's death cut through his alcohol haze somewhat, if not enough to correct the way he was allowing the car to meander from one side of the road to the other.

'... whether there is any point in selecting a successor at all. Meanwhile, two additional items of news concerning the SPOIL crisis are coming in. Sister Kathleen of Delhi, who has won the admiration of the world for her work among the poor on the Indian subcontinent, has let it be known she has SPOIL. Her intention, she says, is to carry on working as long as possible.

'And in the United States evangelist Mason Dexter has been reported missing. Indications are that a substantial sum of money, collected at mass rallies at which he claimed to pass on the SPOIL strain, may be unaccounted for. There are unconfirmed reports that a number of his associates are under arrest pending an inquiry by the FBI.

'We'll have more on these stories in our nine o'clock bulletin.'

Harris burped loudly, accelerated, and strained to focus on the road ahead.

Sheila was in her local supermarket when it happened.

A woman, around thirty, a wire basket over one arm, was queuing at the delicatessen counter. The evidence of SPOIL marking her features, although an increasingly common sight on the streets, still drew the occasional stare. A small knot of shoppers, laden trolleys parked to one side of an aisle, punctuated their gossip with peeks in the woman's direction. But they quickly averted their gaze whenever it seemed she might notice.

It was quite sudden and totally unexpected.

Sheila, rummaging in a deep-freeze compartment, was brought up short by a loud crash. Looking for the source, she saw the woman had dropped her basket and, absolutely still, was pressing her forehead against the glass top of the counter. Her breathing became a rapid pant, like a dog with sunstroke. People around her, obeying the peculiarly English impulse not to get involved, were edging away.

The tableau remained in place for what seemed like an eternity. Then the woman quivered, a heaving of her shoulders first, followed by waves of involuntary shivers running the length of her body.

Sheila approached, anxious to help. But also curious, if she were being honest. The small crowd moved further back. An assistant, sporting a badge that declared he was, irrespective of youth and acne, the deputy manager, appeared from the front of the store. But he held off too, looking uncertain as to how to handle the situation.

At the woman's back now, no one else within ten yards of them, Sheila gingerly reached out and lightly touched her shoulder. There was no immediate reaction. As she was about to try again, the woman turned.

The look on her face, while by no means grotesque or threatening – indeed as far from these as could be – nevertheless made Sheila involuntarily move back. If it were possible for a face to wear an expression of serenity so intense, so all-embracing and unmistakable, that was what her countenance conveyed.

Slowly, silently, and with what Sheila could only think of as nobility, despite the bizarre circumstances, the woman sank to her knees, her look of ecstasy unwavering.

Sheila knew what was about to come, but could not have moved away if her life depended on it. She wondered how many of the others present, most of them mute and rooted with fascination, had any idea of what the last stage involved.

It began.

The woman, slumped in a tangled approximation of the lotus position, started to sway back and forth, imperceptibly at first, then gathering momentum.

After a moment she stopped, arms flopping, the sound of

her knuckles cracking the tiled floor clearly audible in the quiet expectancy.

The air above and around her head shimmered like heat over tarmac on a summer's day. Gradually, so gradually Sheila was at first doubtful it was actually occurring, a gentle bluish light appeared to pulse faintly along the woman's body. The look of rapture remained fixed upon her face as her skin took on an appearance of milky translucency.

There was no denying the throbbing light now, alternating white and electric blue, its intensity growing with each beat. What looked like ghostly flames ringed the woman's figure. Momentarily Sheila was reminded of those newsreels of Buddhists who burnt themselves to death in protest at the Vietnam War.

But it was a bad analogy. This was infinitely more awesome.

There were audible gasps – perhaps including Sheila's own, she couldn't tell – and a squeaky scream came from somewhere behind. The radiance built and built, pounding with an almost physical force, as a sparkling, multicoloured semicircle formed itself around the crown of the woman's head. The spaces between the rhythm of luminescence grew shorter.

Then a blinding glory.

In the nano-second before, Sheila thought she could make out something in the heat of the throbbing inferno of light, something that seemed to rise and move away from the shell of the crumpled body.

It was beautiful.

Someone was laughing, semi-hysterically.

Sheila peered through the dazzle playing before her eyes. The dead woman was whole, complete, untouched. More: the stigmata of SPOIL, for that was how Sheila had come to regard it, was gone. Only the grimace of bliss remained.

For hours afterwards she had stinging floats on her retinas, as though she had been staring into the sun.

'Mrs Veronica Flint, founder and director of the Morality Now organisation, was killed in a car crash this evening. Her Ford Fiesta was in collision with another car at a junction in Upper Sydenham, South East London. Mrs Flint died instantly. The other driver, who police say was well over the alcohol limit and not wearing a seat belt, died of his injuries later in hospital. Mrs Flint is survived by her husband, Andrew, and seven children.

'She will be remembered for her work with the pro-life movement and tireless campaigning against pornography, underage sex and homosexual practices, which she regarded as essentially anti-Christian. Mrs Flint was forty-eight, and is believed not to have had SPOIL.

'Now here is a SPOIL update. There were seven hundred and sixty four notified deaths from the disease in the London area alone yesterday. The Department of Health reminds people that the crisis is stretching the medical and emergency services to the limit. In view of this, you are advised not to expect an immediate response from the emergency services. If a member of your family dies, the DoH says, wrap them in a blanket or sheet...'

Sheila sat by the window in her flat at the Barbican, the lights out, a glass of white wine in her hand.

She remembered something Gerald Sterling said that had made her laugh, after the Forum broadcast. He was actually quite nice, and she warmed to his irreverent humour, despite their different world views. They were talking about SPOIL, of course, and she got him to put his preconceptions aside and speculate on God's purpose. Gerald said he was born a Jew, and rejected the faith in his early twenties, but he frequently remembered something his grandmother used to say when he was a boy. Whenever he asked her why God didn't intervene in the world and put right its many injustices, she would always quote an old Hebrew adage. If God lived on Earth, she said, people would break his windows.

Sheila hadn't bothered to go into the office today, and wasn't surprised when nobody rang about it. Things were falling apart fast now. It was as though some kind of event horizon had been reached, with the number of SPOIL cases overwhelming

82

the system.

As if on cue far off in the darkened streets below an intense, lightning-like flash flickered and died. Almost immediately another caught her eye in one of the apartment blocks opposite, briefly illuminating the interior of someone's living room.

God's firework display. She giggled. They had been flaring up all over town ever since darkness fell, and at first she toasted each one, before realising their quantity far out-numbered her capacity for drink.

It was funny how things like Gerald's quote came back to you. In her case it was something the nuns got her to memorise when she was a girl, a passage from Thessalonians : "For the Lord himself will come down from heaven, with a loud command, with the voice of the archangel and the trumpet call of God, and the dead in Christ will rise first."

Well, not much in the way of loud commands or trumpet calls so far, but things were certainly livening up down here on Earth. About an hour ago she had seen a large mob of people milling around outside St Paul's. The cathedral had been locked and there was a thin line of policemen trying to stop them getting in. It was pretty ugly, with people shouting and waving sticks, but somehow the scene didn't frighten her the way it once would have.

Of course, things were different now. She lifted her wrist and looked at the sores developing there, knew there were several coming up nicely on her face too. When the bouts of sickness had hit her a couple of days ago she had hardly dared hope, but it looked as though she hadn't been forgotten.

She tried not to feel smug about it.

The Time of the Gathering, the Bible called it. She remembered that. The Harvest of the Earth. Although in the event God seemed to have come up with a slow Armageddon.

Gerald had said something else. What was it? Oh yes. He'd said, "If SPOIL is God's doing, what's the Devil up to?" That was a funny thing to say. Still, theology wasn't his strong point, not surprisingly. Sheila felt quite sorry for him really.

She poured herself another drink and settled back to watch the churches burning.

Throwing A Wobbly

The bumblebee wheezed.

At least, that's what it sounded like to Vaughan Cramer. But, being only half awake and fully hungover, he wasn't sure.

He blinked into the shaft of watery sunlight cleaving the window and ran his tongue over arid lips. The experience compared to staring at a searchlight point blank while rubbing his mouth with emery cloth.

Can *insects wheeze?* he wondered sluggishly.

Probably not. But the way things had gone recently he was prepared to believe anything.

Cramer shifted slightly. An empty vodka bottle rolled from the bed and met the carpet with a silken thud. He winced. Pain was an inadequate word to describe what was going on inside his head.

The bumblebee resembled a black and orange striped ping-pong ball decorated with pipe cleaners. It looked far too heavy for something as ambitious as flight. The simple act of walking seemed to present it with a major challenge. So how the hell it got into the flat and on to the windowsill was a mystery.

He watched the insect's repeated attempts to climb the side of a flowerpot. Each time it started to crawl up, weight and exhaustion sent it sliding back down. Its continuous buzzing could have passed for the sound made by an electric shaver. Above, and just beyond reach, the corpulent plant sagged with excess mass, bloated stalks drooping.

Losing interest, he groped for the TV remote control in folds of bedclothes. He punched a channel and muted the sound. At the bottom of the screen the time and date display read *07.53 – E+122.*

A film clip showed a busy street. Obese people were struggling to mount a bus. In the background stout rush hour travellers waddled to work. This was replaced by footage of a protest meeting. Thousands of grossly proportioned demonstrators were crammed into what he took to be Trafalgar Square. Ample arms held aloft placards and banners. Another scene appeared. A fat man with the unmistakable air of a politician, in a smart if bulging three-piece suit, pontificated silently from behind an imposing mahogany desk.

Then it was back to the studio. Presenters Ricki and Jodie filled the famous couch, wedged together so tightly they gave the impression of being joined at their beefy forearms, like overweight Siamese twins. Rigid grimaces fixed on their plump faces, they were going through the morning papers, indicating garish tabloid headlines with fingers akin to pork sausages. She had all the grace and elegance of a barrage balloon. He was sweating freely.

Cramer almost smiled. There wasn't much to be said in favour of the present situation but at least it was democratic. As with death and taxes, there were no exceptions.

Or none proven, he reminded himself.

He was taking in the ungainly spectacle of a vast TV weather girl obscuring her map when a banshee wailed. It kept on until he strained for the phone on his bedside table.

Before he could croak a greeting, his caller boomed, *'Cramer? Biddlecombe!'*

'Sir?' he mumbled, throat parched, head throbbing.

Biddlecombe got straight to the point. *'You've got an assignment. And I want you in situ ASAP.'* His manner was crisp, strident, authoritative. As usual.

'But, uhm, it's my day off,' Cramer protested weakly. 'I had leave owing, remember, and –'

'We're in the throes of a national emergency, Cramer, a triple red alert scenario. I shouldn't have to remind you of that.'

'No, but –'

'Everyone's expected to do their bit and you're no exception.'

'Of course, and normally I'd –'

'None of the other *field operatives would* dream *of taking time off in the current circumstances.'*

'I'm sure they –'

'All hands to the pump, shoulders to the wheel, your country expects, that kind of thing.'

Cramer sighed and gave in. 'What exactly do you want me to do, sir?' he offered meekly.

'There's been another tip-off from a member of the public. You're the only chap we can spare, and as it happens the incident took place not far from you.'

'If it took place at all,' Cramer muttered.

'What? Speak up!'

'Just commenting on the unreliability of these so-called sightings, sir.'

'No need to remind me how untrustworthy civilians can be in such matters. We both know our success rate has been less than substantial. '

'It's been less than anything at all as I understand it, sir. Zero, nil, naught –'

'Yes, thank you, Cramer; I'm well aware of our lack of headway. As are the cabinet and top brass, not to mention the media. Which is all the more reason to investigate every case. Now take down the details.'

Cramer fumbled for a notebook and pen.

Once that was over, Biddlecombe signed off with a hearty, *'Good show! I'll expect your report no later than fifteen hundred hours, in person.'*

The line went dead.

Cursing, Cramer hung up and tossed the notebook aside. Now he couldn't spend the day with Melanie, as he'd promised, and her big event was this afternoon. But if he really moved he might be able to see her briefly on his way back.

There was coverage of an athletics meeting on the TV. Elephantine "runners" lumbered around the track at a snail's pace. The scene cut to a rotund javelin thrower. Abundant flesh barely constrained by tortured lycra, he managed to break into an amble. Feebly, he lobbed his spear. It landed an arm's length in front of him. He collapsed, gasping.

Cramer killed the picture and began easing out of bed. It creaked ominously.

Clutching the adjacent table for support, he slowly manoeuvred his massive, quivering bulk into a standing position. As he did so he caught a glimpse of himself in the wall mirror. Shuddering, he was reminded of why he got so drunk the previous evening. After pausing a few seconds to regain his breath, he was ready for the plod to the kitchen.

At the door, perspiration sheened and puffing, he stopped and glanced at the windowsill. The bumblebee was still trying to climb the pot.

It went up, it bumped down. Went up, bumped down. Up. Down.

He could have sworn he heard it pant.

It was going to be a warm day, damn it.

Cramer stood outside his apartment block, patting his pockets for car keys. Black coffee and analgesics had taken the edge off his hangover but he was far from comfortable. His head was full of shattered crystal and his fresh clothes were already sweaty.

A posh-looking woman shambled by. She wore a dress the size of a marquee. But a *designer* marquee. It was still possible to detect a remnant of her sophisticated beauty, now sabotaged by layers of fat. A lead attached her to a small breed of dog, maybe a pug, although the word small was purely academic. As sour-faced as its mistress, the animal was equally obese. Its short legs were immense and bowed, its distended belly scraped the pavement.

Further along the street a huge traffic warden leaned on a parking meter, gulping air. Once again it occurred to Cramer that a bizarre kind of equality had been imposed.

He found the keys and unlocked his car. In common with

most vehicles still on the road, his had been customised to meet the new requirements. The chassis and axle were reinforced. All but the driver's seat had been removed, and that was set well back. Even so, he had trouble squeezing into it.

Having mopped his brow with a handkerchief, he checked the address and started out. By necessity, his speed was low.

So were his spirits. The frustration at having to change his plans and disappoint Melanie was sharpened by the feeling that he was about to investigate a false alarm or hoax. Just like all the others.

He passed a trio of joggers. Two women and a man, decked out in voluminous track suits, any of them could have doubled as a primary coloured blimp. Not that they were likely to be called upon to perform such a task. The women each held one of the man's arms and were gently steering him toward a bench. He was ashen faced, breathless from over-exertion.

Cramer allowed himself to drive a little faster and snapped on the radio.

'... *leading health food manufacturer Weightanull brings you Slimofast, the revolutionary new aid to weight reduction. Have the benefits of slimming supplements and strenuous regimes proved too* thin *for your liking? Are you* fed up *with faddish diets?* Tired *of tedious exercise? Then look no further! Because Slimofast is* guaranteed *to work!*'

A chorus of what appeared to be demented chipmunks warbled,

'*Slim-o-fast, Slim-o-fast,*
makes those pounds melt off at last.
Slim-o-fast, Slim-o-fast,
now your flab's a thing of the past.'

'*Yes, Slimofast, the miracle weight-loss tonic.* Proven *effective and* entirely *safe. Slimofast, enriched with age-old wonder ingredients including Tibetan yak's spleen, ground bark from South America's bungo-bango tree and —*'

Cramer hit the off button and expelled a weary breath.

Grimly, he concentrated on the traffic.

The house was a modest semi, tucked away at the end of Blackhorse Avenue and overlooking the woods fringing Dickens Heath.

As Cramer shoe-horned himself out of the car a paper boy staggered past, hefty orange shoulder bag adding to his gigantic girth. He sported the *de rigueur* sullen expression of teenage and a baseball cap that adorned his head like an egg cup balanced on a pumpkin. However much material had been lavished on constructing his trousers didn't stop them riding above ankles of mammoth circumference.

Cramer went through the gate and trudged along the path. He rang the doorbell.

While he waited he cast an eye over the lawn's fleshy blades of grass and the chubby plants choking the borders. Fat ants meandered languidly across the paving stones.

It was getting warmer. He loosened his tie.

The door was eventually opened by an elderly man huffing from the effort of reaching it. He was built like a tank, of course.

'Yes?' he panted.

'Mr Jarvis?'

The man nodded.

'S.I.D.,' Cramer announced.

Jarvis thought about that for a moment. 'That's Sid, isn't it?'

'Er, if you like.'

'What about it?'

Cramer was mystified. 'What about what?'

'Sid.'

'That's why I'm here.'

'There's nobody called Sid here, mate. Try number thirty-six.'

'No, no, *I'm* Sid... I mean S.I.D.'

'Well what you doing coming here asking for yourself then?' He gave Cramer the sort of look people reserved for lunatics.

'You don't understand,' Cramer insisted. 'I'm here because

I'm *S.I.D.*'

'I can spell Sid you know,' Jarvis informed him indignantly, 'I'm not stupid.'

'I'm with S.I.D.!' Cramer persisted.

'Oh, so now you're *with* this Sid, are you?' Jarvis scanned the street. 'Where is he?'

Cramer considered punching him. Instead he said, 'Let's start again, shall we?' He fished out his ID card and shoved it under the man's bulbous nose. 'My name is Vaughan Cramer and I'm a representative of the Home Office's Special Investigations Department.' He added slowly and deliberately, 'S.I.D.'

'I don't know why you couldn't have said that in the first place,' Jarvis sniffed.

A woman appeared in the hallway behind him. She was about his age and of corresponding immensity.

'Who is it, Raymond?' she called.

'Bloke from the Home Office,' he told her. 'Says his name's Sid Vaughan-Cramer.'

Cramer decided not to argue.

'Don't keep him standing at the door,' the woman reproved, 'ask him in.'

'The wife,' Jarvis explained ruefully, jabbing a meaty thumb in her direction. 'Nora.'

There followed a moment's awkwardness as Cramer negotiated his way past Jarvis and into the house.

A bird cage hung from a stand in the living room. An incredibly obese budgerigar lay palpitating in it. Nora Jarvis tinged the bars with her finger and cooed, 'Joey? Joey, Joey, Joey. Fancy a nice bit of cuttlefish, Joey?'

Other than the rise and fall of his vast feathery chest, Joey did not react.

They solemnly decamped to the three-piece suite. The furniture groaned.

Cramer produced his notebook and flipped through the pages. 'As you know,' he began, 'I'm here because you called to report a Pref.'

'Is this to get the reward?' piped up Mr Jarvis.

'Ah, well, that isn't my –'

'All the advertisements say there's a reward for reporting this kind of thing,' Mrs Jarvis interjected.

'The reward's payable against proof,' Cramer pointed out.

'Oh.' She shared her husband's look of disappointment.

'It's my job to get that proof,' Cramer went on, 'and if I find it, you'll be in line for the reward.'

'So what do we have to do?' Mr Jarvis asked.

'Just answer my questions.'

'We did all that on the phone.'

'Bear with me while I go over some points, okay?'

They nodded, glumly. The action set their glistening jowls juddering.

'I understand you reported the incident as taking place last night.'

'That's right,' Mrs Jarvis confirmed. 'About ten-thirty.'

'And it was here?'

Mr Jarvis pointed to the French windows and the back garden outside. 'Yes, over there.'

At the end of the garden was a low fence. Beyond that, an incline swept up to a wooded area on the edge of the heath.

'What happened?' Cramer prompted.

'We were watching television. Nora went to draw the curtains and called me to come and look at something.'

'What exactly did you see?'

'One of *them*,' Mrs Jarvis said. 'A Pref. Bold as brass, standing by that big tree.' She indicated a swollen oak.

'Male or female?'

'I didn't know trees had sexes.'

'The *Pref*,' Cramer clarified.

They both agreed it was a woman.

'Young,' Mrs Jarvis added.

'What was she doing?'

'Doing? Nothing. Just standing there. Then after a couple of minutes she spotted us and ran off into the woods.'

'I see. Was there anything unusual about her appearance?'

'She was a *Pref*,' Mr Jarvis replied. 'I'd say that was unusual enough, wouldn't you?'

'I mean any particular physical characteristics. Anything out of the ordinary.'

'Don't think so. Mind you, we were pretty shocked at seeing her at the bottom of our garden, so I don't suppose we took it all in. We called the police, naturally.'

'But they drew a blank?'

'They fannied about out there for an hour or so, but didn't find anything.'

'And this is the first time you've seen her? Or any other Pref around here?'

'Oh, yes,' Mrs Jarvis told him. 'We'd have called earlier if that was the case. You can't be in for the reward if you don't call, can you?'

'We've never had any luck on the lottery,' Mr Jarvis stated, 'but maybe we'll do better with this.'

So much for civic duty, Cramer thought.

He closed the notebook. 'Well, that's all I need. Thank you for your help.' Heaving himself to his feet, he shook their hands.

'My pleasure, Sid,' Mr Jarvis beamed.

As Cramer was leaving, the budgie achieved a pathetic tweet.

It hadn't taken him long to investigate the site, and he wasn't surprised not to have found anything. Although precisely *what* Biddlecombe and the Department thought constituted evidence had always puzzled him. Nothing short of a real live Pref, presumably.

Yeah, and the Loch Ness monster and Bigfoot thrown in for good measure, he reflected cynically.

Traffic in the city centre was busier than when he left, and he was worried about parking. But when he got to the multistorey car park the green *Spaces* sign was lit up.

There were pigeons sauntering in the slip road leading to the entrance. They were too fat to fly. It was nice to see one thing that hadn't changed.

Having scattered them with his horn, he had to drive up several floors to find a bay. Which presented the problem of getting down again. In his condition the stairs weren't an attractive option. The queue waiting to use the tiny lift was hardly more appealing. There were new laws about the number of people who could ride a lift together, but many ignored them, often with disastrous consequences. Cramer chose the stairs.

Twenty minutes later he emerged at ground level. Bushed. Then came the futility of trying to find a taxi. With walking too difficult for so many people, and the recent one passenger only rule, cabs were gold dust. In the end he gave up and set out for Melanie's show on foot.

The amount of time he had left before having to report to HQ was trickling away. But he contained his irritation and kept to a moderate pace. It was hot, and he saw more than one small crowd clustered around a porcine pedestrian downed by heat stroke. He didn't want to be one of them.

Eventually, dishevelled and flustered, he arrived at the Royal Fortescue hotel.

Even as the mountainous doorman directed a lethargic salute at him, sounds of a commotion came from the building's revolving doors. Several hulking guests, with luggage, had unwisely entered at the same time. More people crowded in behind them and the mechanism had jammed.

The interior of the no-longer-spinning doors was a tableaux of compacted flesh. Faces squashed against the glass in grotesque imitation of gaping goldfish. Pudgy hands pressured the panes. A cacophony of muffled woe arose.

Roused from sloth to mere indolence, the flunky clumped to the rescue. He tugged mightily at the brass rail on the door. It wouldn't budge. The muted whimpers of outrage within cranked up a couple of notches.

Liveried employees appeared, several pushing from inside, others pulling with the doorman. Their task was made no easier by the trapped guests, who were pulling and pushing against their would-be saviours. The entire structure shook precariously, then suddenly freed itself.

The captives squirted out, disgorged like lumpy toothpaste from a stomped tube. They were deposited on the hotel's forecourt in a tangled heap of blubbery limbs and ruptured suitcases. An unseemly fracas ensued.

In his mind, Cramer chalked up the score. Flubber: 1, Dignity: 0.

He skirted the melee and entered the hotel by a side door.

A sign in the lobby read –

An Extravaganza of Summer Couture
New Season's Fashions for the Fuller Figure
Exclusive Preview —>

He went the way indicated and produced his invitation for a colossal young woman in a black mini dress. Smiling, she waved him into the hall.

It was packed with an audience of cultured, affluent and universally titanic potential buyers. A very gratifying turn-out for his girlfriend's first major appearance.

Cramer's seat was in the first row on one side of the catwalk extending from the flower-bedecked stage. By the time he elbowed his way to it the lights were dimming and rhythmic music pounded.

The show began. A parade of youthful, grossly overweight models wiggled, tottered and gyrated through a ponderous routine that set the catwalk bouncing. They regaled the spectators with expansive trouser suits, boundless frocks, abundant two-piece outfits and swimwear assembled from measureless quantities of textile. Fortified high-heels, huge wedged clogs and boat-like sandals tramped the boards.

When Melanie eventually appeared she was decked out in a plentiful white ball gown, glittering with pastel sequins. Her lengthy chestnut coloured hair cascaded freely. Drawing level with Cramer she grinned and gave him a coquettish wink.

Notwithstanding multiple chins, stevedore's arms and tree trunk legs, she was beautiful.

At the finale all the models gathered on the catwalk together, bathing in the audience's applause. Then the French designer, Jean-Michel Grandpierre, made a dramatic entrance. An unmistakable figure, resplendent in his trademark kilt, platinum hair cropped, the Gallic sartor blew kisses to his admiring public and pecked the models' generous cheeks.

As the clapping died down he waddled to the microphone.

'Ladeez and genteelmean,' he intoned, 'I fank you for attendean my liddle show zis aftarnoon.'

Amid the smattering of rekindled applause, Cramer thought he heard something resembling the groan of yielding wood.

'I must alsow fank all zee boyz and gurlz ear on stage wiff me...'

The sound repeated itself, slightly louder and more prolonged.

'... wiffout ume all zis would 'ave been... 'ow you zay...? not pozibale.'

There was another, even more pronounced noise; a cross between a creak and a crack. No one on the catwalk seemed to notice, though several people in the audience were looking anxious.

'I shood alzo zay a beeg fank you to zee peeple in zee beckgroom for zere...'

A sharp *snap!* rang out, loud as a pistol shot.

'... 'ard work and... *Sacre bleu!*

The catwalk lurched violently. Several of the models issued alarmed squeaks. Grandpierre desperately clutched the microphone stand.

For an eternal second, time froze.

Then with a thunderous roar the platform collapsed.

Models went down like poleaxed hippopotami. The Frenchman landed on his well-padded bottom, revealing the full extent of his monstrous legs. And graphically illustrated that, despite the kilt, he did not embrace Scottish customs in *all* matters sartorial.

Chaos reigned. There were shrieks, shouts and screams; large tracts of flesh were exposed. Dust billowed.

Cramer was one of the first members of the audience to timorously scale the wreckage. Heart thumping, he hurried to Melanie as fast as his cumbersome bulk allowed. She was already sitting up, a bemused expression on her face.

'Are you... all... right?' he gasped, plonking down beside her.

'Think so.' She flicked locks of hair away from her eyes with a ham fist. 'How are the others?'

He looked around. Several people had hold of Grandpierre's arms and were straining to hoist him upright. None of the models seemed seriously hurt.

'I'd say pride was the main casualty.' He attempted the impossible task of putting an arm around her shoulders. 'Sure you're okay?'

She nodded. 'But I wouldn't mind getting out of here. Will you help me up so I can go and change?'

He almost strained his back before a posse of bellhops came and lent him a hand.

They didn't have time for much more than a coffee together. A woman at an adjoining table was tucking into numerous rich cakes, ice cream sundaes and milk shakes. As weight apparently couldn't be lost by any means, whatever the slimming industry claimed, some people had taken it as a licence to scoff.

Before he had to leave, Cramer swore he'd spend the day with Melanie on her birthday, E+127, even if it meant feigning illness to get off work. When he asked her what she'd like for a present she said, 'Anorexia nervosa.'

They both wished it was that easy.

Having arranged to see each other again the next evening, Cramer headed for S.I.D. headquarters in Whitehall.

He was nearly late for the appointment. His watch, with the specially extended strap, showed just four minutes to spare. Once through Security, the receptionist said he was expected in the basement gymnasium.

Dozens of S.I.D. personnel were down there, weight-lifting, practicing aerobics, jabbing punchbags and engaged in all manner of other clumsy and hopeless bids at fat reduction.

Cramer found Biddlecombe stuffed in some torturous exercise machine. He was red-faced and oozing perspiration. It was obvious he was relieved at Cramer's arrival because it meant he could stop punishing himself. Not that he would ever admit to that.

'Ah... Cramer,' he gasped. 'You should... try... some... of this... yourself.'

'No disrespect, chief, but I don't see the point. Nothing seems to work, so why waste the time?'

'Nonsense.' Biddlecombe was still pooped but getting his breath back. 'It's... wonderful. Very... character-building.'

'Doesn't shift the weight though, does it, sir?'

'That's no reason... not to try,' his boss huffed, neat grey moustache bristling with irritation. 'I'm thinking of making it... compulsory for... the whole department, in fact.'

Cramer didn't relish *that* prospect, but held his tongue.

'I'll be right with you,' Biddlecombe said, beckoning a pair of overblown attendants.

Once they levered him out of the contraption he stepped on a set of scales. His face darkened.

'Any improvement?' Cramer inquired innocently.

Biddlecombe's wordless glare was eloquent enough an answer.

When his boss had changed from track suit to the more

familiar pinstripes, he lead the way to a lift. Even with just the two of them inside it felt terribly cramped.

As they ascended, Biddlecombe said, 'What's your verdict on that sighting?'

'Probably just another dead end. No proof of any kind beyond witnesses out for the reward. And if it isn't money-seekers it's nuts or sensationalists. These reports are turning out to be about as substantial as UFOs.'

'*They've* risen too, you know, according to the Defence Ministry.'

'Doesn't surprise me, sir. People are looking for answers.'

'Yes, not least the PM. I had a meeting with him this morning to deliver a progress report. *Progress* report indeed!'

'We haven't exactly had a lot of that, have we, sir?'

'Precious little. As the Premier never tires of pointing out. Which is why I need results!'

Cramer noticed that they were halfway between the fourth and fifth floors.

'Where are we going, sir?' he ventured to ask.

'Press conference. With the bloody reptiles in a feeding frenzy again, no doubt. You'll be representing the field operatives.'

'*Me? A press conference?* But... but... but...'

'You sound like an outboard motor,' Biddlecombe barked. 'What's the problem, man?'

'I... I've never answered questions from the Press before, sir. I mean, I wasn't warned or –'

'Don't be a complete prawn, Cramer. Apart from me, Norbreck's going to be there, and we'll do most of the talking. You're just to make up the numbers. Should any of the hacks ask you anything, all you have to do is remember you're subject to the Official Secrets Act, smile like an idiot and tell 'em everything's under control. That's what I always do.'

Oh God, Cramer thought.

The lift tinged, its doors slid open and they spilled out.

Walking to the suite set aside for media briefings, Cramer felt like a condemned man.

All the chairs in the press room were occupied. In many cases, several were filled by the same person. They faced a low dais supporting a trestle table covered in a white tablecloth and festooned with microphones. Norbreck was seated there already. Biddlecombe and Cramer joined him. As they settled, three camera crews moved in and jostled for best position.

Staring out at the rows of tubby, unsmiling faces, Cramer quaked.

Biddlecombe nudged him in the vicinity of his well-buried ribs. *'Smile,'* he hissed.

Cramer adopted a deranged smirk.

His boss raised a hand. 'Let's begin, shall we?' The room quietened. 'Most of you know me, but for those who don't, I'm George Biddlecombe, General Administrative Secretary, Special Investigations Department. On my left is government Chief Scientist Professor Langley Norbreck.'

The burgeoning boffin favoured them with a laid-back, 'Afternoon.'

'And on my right,' Biddlecombe continued, 'is Vaughan Cramer, one of the Department's investigating officers.'

Cramer said, 'Uhnga. Omfh.'

Biddlecombe cleared his throat. 'We won't bore you with prepared statements today, ladies and gentlemen; we'll just answer any questions you may have.'

A forest of podgy hands went up. Biddlecombe pointed at one.

'Adrian Shelley, Daily Dispatch. Does that mean you haven't anything worth telling us?'

'Not at all. Next!'

'Dominic Moody, The Defender. Can you outline exactly what progress has been made in understanding the nature of the present emergency?'

'I think that one's best answered by Professor Norbreck,'

Biddlecombe responded. 'Professor?'

Norbreck leaned back in his protesting chair. 'We have made *some* advances in our knowledge, but it's early days yet. Remember, it's only about four months since the event that has come to be known as the Enlargement took place. However, several facts have been established.' He counted them off on chunky fingers. 'One, we know that the Enlargement occurred in a single twenty-four hour period, arriving with the rising sun and fully establishing itself by sunset. Two, this is a global phenomenon. Three, the condition affects all lifeforms; humans, animals, insects, plants, even organisms on a microbiological level. There appear to be no exceptions.'

'What about the Prefs?' an unshaven, shambolic character in the first row shouted. '*They're* exceptions, ain't they?' As an afterthought, he identified himself. 'Eddie Squallor, The Comet.'

Biddlecombe took over. 'Ah, Mr Squallor. Forthright as ever in representing the concerns of the... *popular* press.' He looked as if he had a bad smell under his nose. 'The issue of Prefs, or Prefatories to give them their full nomenclature, is subject to detailed and thorough investigation.'

'Nom-what?' Squallor muttered.

Another reporter hoisted himself up. 'Osbert Rayner, Globe and Telegraph. Perhaps you could fill us in on the results of this "detailed and thorough investigation".'

For the first time, Biddlecombe seemed ill at ease. 'It's a situation we're keeping constantly under review. To say more than that at the moment could jeopardise national security.'

There was uproar.

'What about the public's right to know?' someone yelled.

'Give us the facts!' demanded another.

'"Fatties Ministry Mandarins in Cover-Up Scandal"!' Squallor exclaimed.

Cramer cringed.

The film crews turned their cameras on the clamouring journos.

'Please! *Please*, ladies and gentlemen!' Biddlecombe pleaded. 'Let's conduct ourselves with some measure of decorum!'

The room eventually calmed down enough for another question.

'Nancy Wakefield, Daily Tribune and Telegraph. The government offers a reward for information about Prefs. How often has the reward been claimed?'

'I don't have the exact figure in front of me,' Biddlecombe stalled, 'but claims run to many hundreds.'

Even in his state of terror, Cramer appreciated the cleverness of his boss' answer. Hundreds of *claims*, yes. Pay-outs were another matter. He reached for a glass of water.

'Grant Edmonds, Evening Bugle News Herald Chronicle Recorder.' He grinned sheepishly. 'Sorry, there's been a lot of mergers lately. It'd be interesting to hear from someone with first-hand experience of investigating Pref sightings. What's your assessment, Mr Cramer?'

Cramer spluttered a fine shower of water over the camera crews. Hands shaking, he slowly returned his glass to the table. 'Pa-pa-pardon?' he stammered.

'The Prefs,' Edmonds repeated. 'It's obviously important to track down any that might exist, but it seems S.I.D. are having certain difficulties in that respect. What do you have to say about it?'

'Umm.' He felt his face turning fiery red. 'Well, I aah... Yes. Definitely.'

'Yes what?' Edmonds persisted.

'Yes it's... important.' He hiccuped . "Scuse me. It's very important... to... look for Preps, er *Prefs*. Yes. *Hic!* 'Scuse.'

'And how many have you found, personally?'

Biddlecombe kicked his shin. '*Ouch!* I mean... hic...! beg pardon. Well, you have to... *hic...!* appreciate that this kind of investi... *hic...!* gation is very difficult and... *hic...!*'

'Hold your breath!' Squallor suggested.

'... Wha –? Oh, right.' Cramer inhaled, filling his lungs and expanding his cheeks hamster fashion.

Biddlecombe snapped shut his gaping jaw and stepped into the breach. 'I think that, er, my colleague Mr Cramer here admirably demonstrates the... dedication... yes, the *dedication* to duty that characterises all Special Investigations Department employees.'

Cramer's eyes began to bulge.

'And let me make clear,' Biddlecombe went on, 'that even as we speak the best scientific minds in the country are engaged in intensive research to solve the mystery of the Enlargement. Be assured that everything that *can* be done *is* being done.'

Cramer was turning blue.

'It remains only to thank you all for coming,' he continued hastily, 'and to gratefully acknowledge the assistance of Professor Norbreck...'

'Afternoon, everybody.'

'... and Mr Cramer. And *Mr Cramer.* Cramer! You can *breathe out* now, man!'

'*Paahhwaaaah!*'

'Just a minute!' Squallor protested. 'We haven't finished yet!'

The rest of the press corps echoed him. A general hubbub of complaints broke out.

'Thank you, thank you,' Biddlecombe recited blandly. 'The attendants will see you out.'

At his gesture, security men began clearing the room. The reporters and camera crews were unceremoniously herded into the corridor, their complaints ignored.

When the door finally slammed, Biddlecombe scowled at Cramer. 'A fat lot of good *you* turned out to be.'

'A *fat* lot of...! Oh, very droll, sir. Yes, it did go rather well, didn't it? Do you think any of them noticed I was a bit nervous? *Hic!* 'Scuse me.'

Early the following evening Cramer was still smarting from the chewing-out his boss had given him.

Sitting in his flat with Melanie, watching himself on TV, did nothing to make him feel any better. They were running footage of the press conference, for the umpteenth time, and it included glimpses of his gauche screen persona.

'Make it go away,' he begged. 'I look such a twazer.'

'It's not *that* bad, Vaughan,' Melanie lied. 'But maybe you're just not cut out to be a performer.' She switched channels.

'*... and I tell you, brothers and sisters, that fat is* good!' a televangelist raved. *'It's good because God willed it! And if any of you out there are foolish enough to find a way of shedding those heaven-sent pounds, you should get down on your knees and tell the Lord, "Forgive me, Father, for I have thinned"!'*

Melanie switched again.

'*... find the lover of your dreams with Heavy Date magazine, the largest circulation contact...'*

She turned off the set.

'Everybody's getting in on the act,' Cramer grumbled.

'You're really tense, Vaughan. Try to calm down.'

'I am calm.'

'You're about as serene as a combine harvester.' She spread her generous arms. 'Come here.'

He joined her on the floor and they snuggled.

'It's your job,' she said.

'Maybe. But if I don't get back in Biddlecombe's good books that'll be academic. I won't *have* a job. On the other hand, I'm thinking of quitting anyway.'

'Why?'

'It's all so pointless, isn't it? Running around looking for Prefs. Chasing moonfluff.'

'Is it? Moonfluff, I mean. Anyway, you have to do what you think is right.'

'What do *you* think's right?'

'This.' She rested her head on his barrel chest. They stayed that way quietly for a few minutes before she spoke again. 'You know, it's strange, and you'll think I'm mad, but the more time passes the more I'm starting to feel that being fat isn't so bad.'

'Hmmm. It's funny how you can get used to just about anything.'

'It's more than getting used to it. It feels... *right*, somehow.'

Bizarrely, Cramer was surprised to find that struck a chord with him. He was about to tell her so when the phone rang.

It was Biddlecombe.

But he hadn't called to deliver a further dressing-down, as Cramer expected.

His boss didn't bother with formalities. *We have a sighting, which according to our informants is going on right now.'*

Cramer sat up. 'Where?'

'The Fairview Housing Estate.'

'That's –'

'Yes, next to Dickens Common. And we've had five or six calls about it. Get yourself over there now, *and don't bungle this one!'*

Cramer slammed down the phone.

'I'm coming!' Melanie declared. 'No arguments!'

They arrived in their separate cars, to maximise speed, and found a crowd on the street. Several police land rovers were parked nearby.

Holding out his ID, Cramer approached an Inspector. 'What's happening?'

'Didn't I see you on the telly last –'

'Yes, yes! What's *happening?'*

'Right. We've had a number of eyewitness reports of a Pref on the heath. That lad over there seems to have got the best look.'

Cramer lumbered to the spheroid youth in question. 'You were the one who saw the Pref, right?'

'Yeah. 'Ere, weren't you on the –'

'Yes, it was me! Now let's get on with it. Where did you see the Pref?'

'Up the end of the road there, where it runs by the woods.'

'Was it a man or a woman?'

'Woman. Well, girl really.'

'Are you *sure*?'

A battleship of a female butted in. 'Oi, mister. I'm his mum. And my Fabian don't tell no fibs. If he says he saw something, he saw it.'

Cramer felt bad about being snappy. 'Sorry, kid. I didn't mean to talk to you so brusquely.'

Fabian was baffled. 'Brusquely? What, that bloke who made all those kung-fu films?'

The Inspector oozed over to join them. He was holding a radio. It seemed miniscule in the enormity of his fist. 'Some of my men have spotted her,' he reported. 'No more than half a mile from here.'

'Can we get there?'

'In a land rover, yes. Specially reinforced jobs, powerful engines.' He glanced at Melanie. 'But I can only take one passenger, I'm afraid.'

'Don't worry, Vaughan, you go ahead,' she told him. 'Go *on*!'

Cramer and the Inspector poured themselves into the vehicle.

As they sped down the road, the radio crackled with a message. 'Seems we've got some of the local citizenry out there looking for her too,' the policeman related.

'Well, we could probably do with the help.'

'Providing they don't get under our feet.'

They drew in behind a police van at the side of the road, a couple of dozen paces from where the woods loomed darkly.

A sergeant and a gaggle of constables greeted them.

'We've got a fix on the Pref, sir,' the Sergeant reported. 'One of our boys saw her a couple of minutes ago, less than a hundred yards north of here. We're in pursuit.'

'What about the locals?'

'A few of them around, which confuses things a bit.' He nodded at the wood. 'Another thing: there's no way we can get the land rovers through that.'

'So we'll be on foot now, Mr Cramer. Want to leave this to us?'

Cramer was determined to get a result this time. 'No, Inspector. I'm coming with you.'

'Suit yourself.' He dug into his pocket and handed over a flashlight. 'You'll find that useful.'

The sergeant and a constable opened the back of their van. There were a trio of German shepherds inside; great hairy beachballs with stubby legs.

'They still have their sense of smell and tracking skills, Mr Cramer,' the Inspector explained. 'And I think it would be best if you stuck by me.'

The group fanned out into the trees.

It was dark and tangled, and just the occasional muted snatch of chatter from the police radios broke the deathly quiet. They used their torches sparingly, so that only now and again a beam knifed briefly and died.

After trudging sweatily for a few minutes they heard voices, quite close at hand. Several people were shouting. The dogs began to growl, then bark. They strained at their leashes. Cramer saw the glowing disks of flashlights no more than a stone's throw away.

'Come on,' the Inspector urged.

They puffed their way through the twisted undergrowth.

'What chance have we got of catching a Pref on foot?' Cramer said. 'She's got to be able to move faster than we can.' He was fighting for breath.

'More of us. We'll try to surround her.'

They ploughed on.

Minutes later they converged with another group of officers, and a smattering of residents from the estate.

'Which way?' the Inspector demanded, rationing his air with staccato speech.

Shafts of light from numerous torches pointed to a nearby

copse.

'Encircle it,' he ordered.

They all moved toward the clump of trees, some entering frontally, others carrying on to the sides and back.

Cramer and the Inspector crashed through foliage and found the ground within sloped down to a depression. They half slid to its floor, raking their flashlights in a sweeping arc before them.

Stumbling, almost falling once, Cramer got ahead of his companion.

He heard something, quite close by.

And stopped.

It sounded like someone whimpering. A woman.

Cramer ducked under a hanging branch, made his way around an amplified bush and found the Pref.

She was lying on her back, one leg twisted unnaturally. He could see how she'd stumbled on an almost hidden root and taken a fall.

The Inspector caught up with him. Two more men followed. Others, police and civilians, came in from all directions. They turned their torches on her. The glare made her screw up her eyes and raise a hand to shield them.

Somebody whispered, 'We finally got one.'

She was young. And thin. Her arms and legs were slim to the point of skinniness. As she took in draughts of air, ribs showed through the flimsy cloth of her tattered dress. Lank hair trailed over her slender face. She had *cheekbones*. It was a miraculous sight.

Cramer thought she was beautiful. But he didn't mention that to anybody.

Even after they killed her.

We Are For the Dark

Six of the clock ante meridiem, twenty-third day of April, the year of Our Lord 1576.

The dust motes dancing in the beam of watery sunlight made him think of fairies. They set in train the notion of a tale concerning the lives and loves of the fairyfolke, dwelling in their forest domain. He resolved to write down the thought when able.

It came to him that fairies and like elfin beings were more in keeping with the balm of a Summer's night than the chill of an early Spring morn. Yet still he populated the shaft flowing through the chapel window with phantasmagorical creatures of ancient lore, moving gracefully to the tune of unseen pipers. Such were the caprices that paraded regularly upon the dais of his mind.

Summer it may not be, William Shakespeare reflected, but this day held especial magic for him all the same.

Magister Armitage droned on.

Will fidgeted slightly, his lower back numb against the severity of the uncushioned bench. Even after four – no, five years now – his body had not ceased rebelling against the hour at which he was required to present himself for schooling. Absently flicking aside a stray lock of ginger hair, he snuck a glance at Guy Spencer sitting beside him. His friend, and the other boys, some five and twenty in number, were blinking, half awake, as the morning sermon rolled on.

Oblivious to his youthful congregation's discomfort, Head of Masters Geoffrey Armitage continued wading through a passage from the lavishly appointed Bishop's Bible propped before him on the lectern. Will found no fault with the text. His feeling of tedium arose, as ever, from a delivery so long of wind.

Guy caught Will's eye. They fought an urge to giggle.

Armitage's second-in-command, Samuel Gower, standing ramrod straight and rancid-faced beside the row of pews, noticed and sent them a fearsome glare. He brandished his leather strap. The pair sobered and returned their attention frontward.

At last Armitage came to the end of his recitation, urged all to labour hard in the day ahead and reminded them of the virtues of *mens sana in corpore saro*. In clipped tone he dismissed them to break fast.

Outside the chapel the students fell to whispered boisterousness as they walked towards the refectory or made off to gather books and notes for their lessons. Will and Guy took the cloistered way. To their right, beyond the pillars, lay an enclosed grassy square edged with borders just beginning to flower. On the opposite side of the garden an open latticed gate afforded a glimpse of Stratford, already bustling with marketeers.

In common with the other boys, Will and Guy wore tunics of darkest blue, indicating their status as grammar school pupils. The garments were cut from wool, the town's chief bringer of trade and prosperity. Will was musing on whether his companion's modest frame would ever grow to fill his properly when Guy spoke, voice pitched low.

''Tis your birth day, Will. Good health. How doth it feel it to reach your twelfth season?'

Will smiled. 'I own I am not quite giddy with the weight of years. Twelve feels much as eleven did. As you will discover for yourself soon enough.'

They were joined by Daniel Burrage. His was the only brain that, in truth, Will accepted as nearest to equalling his own. Though he had never uttered this opinion.

'Good morrow,' Will greeted. 'Are you game for Virgil this afternoon?'

'A probation of the philosopher's tracts? Aye, I'll match wits with you.'

'And come off second best again, I'll warrant,' Guy opined.

It was meant as gentle raillery and, despite being well known for a humourless disposition, Burrage took it as such.

John Dudley fell in beside them next, shoulders round, gaze downcast. At ten years he was the youngest of their circle.

'You look troubled, John,' Will said. 'What ails you?'

'I know not the Greek we were set,' the child replied miserably, 'nor can I grip the summes.'

'You *can*,' Will assured him. 'You lack not the intellect but the mettle.' He laid a comforting hand on his arm. 'Have faith in yourself.'

'I will be beaten.'

'No, you will prevail.'

As he spoke, they were passed by a sobbing child.

'Methinks that was not best timed,' Guy muttered.

'Nor this,' added Will, nodding toward an approaching figure.

Thomas Nashe swaggered up to them. He was a robust lad, short and stocky, heavy-browed and with a distinct absence of neck.

'Ah, the swats,' he sneered. 'Save you, Dudley, the runt of the litter.'

'If our company be so distasteful, allow us to bid you a heartfelt good riddance,' Will responded.

'Come, come, ill grace doth not befit you on such a day.' His words dripped with sarcasm. ''Tis a time for celebration, I'm told, and doubtless you will be presenting us with one of your verses. To commemorate yourself.'

'Yes, my fancy is to write of the piling years as like a wide, black well that swalloweth all hope. I would take as my inspiration your mouth, Tom.'

Nashe's face darkened ominously.

'Hold,' Daniel interjected. 'What is this?'

They looked in the direction he indicated. On the edge of the lawn, perhaps ten yards away, Samuel Gower stood in close proximity to Nathan Webb, the Bible studies tutor. It was obvious from their intemperate expressions and gestures that they were engaged in an argument.

It ended abruptly with Webb storming away. Then Gower saw the boys staring and headed for them like a vengeful wraith.

He arrived red faced and seething with anger.

'*You!*' he snapped. 'Shakespeare and Spencer. I will broach no disrespect in chapel.' He levelled his strap at them. 'Repeat it and you will feel my sting. And *all* of you will observe the rule of silence when moving about the school. Ignore me at your peril.'

Without further ado, Gower strode off.

None mistook the gravity of his threat. Sharp experience had been their mentor in such matters. As they continued their journey, all, Nashe included, were united in unspoken detestation of the man. Shortly, Nashe departed on an errand of his own. John and Daniel went on ahead, leaving Will and Guy to travel alone to the dining hall.

They were the last to arrive. A master boomed '*privatim et serriatim!*' The crowd of students did as they were told and formed ranks in front of the door. Through it, Will could make out the long, plain wooden tables. They were laid with jugs of water and ale, alongside platters bearing loaves of barley bread, fish, eggs and wedges of pungent cheese.

Having stood in line for several minutes, they were at the point of entering when Armitage appeared from behind. He looked into the hall and tutted.

'No sign of Magister Gower,' he complained, as much to himself as them, 'and he is to lead the blessing afore bread is broken.' He addressed the boys directly. 'Masters Will and Guy. Go with haste and bid my deputy's presence forthwith.'

Will asked, 'Where may we find him, sir?'

'His study would be most fertile a place to begin. Be gone.'

They chorused assent and set off, finding little joy in the prospect.

To reach their destination meant crossing the garden square.

As they trod the spongy grass, Will pointed. 'Look. Tobias Fraser.'

The school gardener, and jack-of-all-trades, was digging in one of the flower beds. Seeing them coming, his countenance brightened. He doffed his cap.

Falteringly he mouthed, 'Good morrow, young masters.'

His pattern of speech, and general aspect, left no doubt that he was a simpleton.

They returned his greeting warmly.

'Still toiling with the fruits of God's bounty, I perceive,' Will commented.

'Aye, master. I am blessed, am I not?'

'That you are, Toby,' Will told him kindly. 'But we beg you forgive our hurry. We carry a message of import.'

Toby grinned. 'Fare thee well then.' He went back to his spade.

''Tis a bitter fate he must bear,' Guy remarked once out of earshot.

'Truly. Though a gentler soul t'would be hard to find. We must remember him when at prayer, friend Guy.'

They arrived at the door of Gower's study. It stood ajar. They knocked. There was no reply. Will called Gower's name, but was rewarded only with silence. He knocked again, with sufficient force that the door swung inward a jot. Deciding the room was empty, they made to leave.

A sound from within halted them. They could not make out what it was. Summoning fortitude, Will entered. Guy followed. The chamber was in darkness, its heavy drapes still undrawn. No candle or lantern burned, although a thin crack of light did penetrate on the far side of the room, where a second door was likewise part ajar.

Calling Gower's name once more brought the noise afresh. Its identity remained elusive.

'A cat, mayhap?' Guy ventured in a whisper.

Will shrugged, mystified.

Leading the way, he moved further into the study. Then he stumbled against some sprawled obstruction, and nearly fell. There was a groan. Alarmed, he bade Guy draw the curtains. The flood of light revealed a dreadful scene.

Gower lay upon the floor, his head a bloody mess.

Both boys let out gasps of horror. The first to gather himself, Will knelt for a closer inspection. It took no great knowledge of the human physique to tell that the man had been savagely battered. But as far as Will could tell, no likely weapon was in sight.

Gower made a sound. Will leaned closer. His lips working feebly, the magister was trying to say something. At length, he managed a single, barely perceptible word. Then a crimson trickle snaked from the corner of his mouth and the death rattle sounded.

Will slowly rose, ashen-faced, and crossed himself.

Guy did likewise and asked 'What did he say?'

'It sounded like... It could only have been... *Fraser.*'

They stared at each other, appalled.

Five and thirty minutes past eight of the clock ante meridiem.

'You are sure that was all he said?' Captain Peregrine Adams asked again.

'Quite sure,' Will repeated. "Twas but the lone word.'

'And you, master Guy? You are certain that the dying man's utterance did not reach your ears?'

'It did not, sir.'

The Captain of the Watch frowned and cast his gaze around those present in the school's smaller lecture room. Apart from the boys and Armitage, they consisted of Nathan Webb, the Bible tutor, Latin master Francis Quincey and Henry Savage, who taught Philosophy.

'You have, what, just above two dozen pupils here, Magister

Armitage?'

'That is correct.'

'And these gentlemen comprise the teaching body?'

'They and one other. We are fortunate in being well-funded by the Church and private benefactors.'

'And the one other of whom you speak?'

'Ambroise Kean, our general factotum. He is currently supervising the boys.'

'Tell me of him.'

'Unlike my colleagues here, who are Oxford men, he is Stratford born and bred, taken on partly through merit, partly out of Christian charity.'

'How so?'

'He was discharged from the Army sore wounded. The affliction left him with a leg all but useless.'

There was a knock at the door.

'Come!' Armitage called.

A member of Adams' Watch entered. He carried a weighty, short-handled hoe. Its iron head was stained with blood.

'I found this, sir,' the man reported, handing over the tool.

Adams inspected it. 'You will observe, gentlemen, not only blood, but on closer examination strands of hair. To my eye, they match the victim's. The murder weapon, no doubt of it.' He nodded at the watchman. 'Good work.'

Will and Guy seemed to have been forgotten. They exchanged surreptitious glances and did nothing to draw attention to themselves.

'Where did you find this?' Adams wanted to know.

'In the lean-to by the gardener's quarters, sir,' the guard replied.

'What more proof is needed?' Francis Quincey exclaimed. 'Gower named his murderer, and now this.'

Adams turned to Armitage. 'Tell me about Tobias Fraser.'

'Another discharged from Her Majesty's service, though of common rank. He was rendered an idiot by a blow to the skull.

There was prospect of him becoming a sturdy beggar if not taken in by us.'

'More Christian charity?'

'Indeed, Captain. We are governed by the principles of High Church and saw it as our duty.'

'He has never given cause for concern,' Nathan Webb intervened.

'Yet his mind is not his own,' Henry Savage countered. 'Who can say what let he has over the demons that torture him?'

Will could contain himself no longer. 'Your pardon, sirs,' he piped-up.

They all looked to him, including Guy, though where their expressions held consternation, his was apprehensive.

'You have something to say, Master Shakespeare?' Armitage answered sternly.

'Tobias Fraser has less malice in his smallest finger than most others have in their entire beings,' Will proclaimed. 'It is beyond reason that he should harm another.'

Armitage came back with asperity. 'We are obliged for your considered opinion, formed as it is by your many years' observation of the human condition.'

Will blushed but persevered. 'It is an impression shared by all who know him.'

'Is that the totality of your measurement of the man, or is there more you would impart?' The head master was now barely containing his displeasure.

'His sweetness of nature best speaks for itself, Magister. But I lay before you one verity. Tobias was at work in the garden scant moments before master Spencer and I came upon the sad scene.'

Adams took up the point. 'And thus could not have committed the atrocity? I think not. There are two doors to Magister Gower's study, both allowing access to different parts of the garden. Fraser could have outpaced you by going the other way. He might have entered the room, done the deed and made his escape before you arrived. Again, he could have undertaken the grisly act *before* you met him.'

'You attribute more guile to him than he is capable of, sir. Moreover, I lay stress on the chance of uncertainty in Magister Gower's dying word. It *sounded* like Fraser, but he was weak —'

'Enough!' Armitage snapped. 'All sensible intelligence points Tobias' way. There is no telling what a man of unsound humours might be capable of. And you, Master Shakespeare, are close to impertinence. You will hold your tongue.'

'It doth seem that the man is most likely culpable,' Adams decided, 'and we must act. But I will use the powers vested in me to order that all, students and masters, must remain confined to these premises for the rest of the day.'

There was a clamour of protest.

'Surely we should close out of respect?' Armitage objected.

'It is possible that Fraser is *not* the culprit,' Adams conceded. 'In which case I want all where none can flee. More of the Watch will be brought to enforce my wish.'

Armitage bristled at this. 'What if the murderer was someone from outside the school, and has already made off?'

'That eventuality is another reason no one should leave. If word spreads through Stratford that a murderer may be loose, my watch will have panic to deal with.'

'I shall appeal to the vicar of Holy Trinity, Jeremiah Rowley. He has ultimate authority over the school.'

'You must do as fit, sir. As a matter of fact I had already sent a man to bring the vicar here, but he cannot be located at present.'

Armitage sighed. 'You will have your way, Captain,' he reluctantly agreed. 'For the time being. But lessons are suspended. In that way at least we can show our respect for Gower. The boys will spend the hours in quiet contemplation and study.'

Adams gave him a stiff head bow. 'I am obliged, Magister. Watchman, arrest this Fraser and take him to the place of incarceration. Have one other with you, lest he prove violent.'

The guard hurried out, grim faced and purposeful.
Will and Guy looked on helplessly.

Eleven of the clock ante meridiem.

The boys had been turned out into the garden square for their mid-morning constitutional, as on any normal day. Ambroise Kean, dragging his withered leg whenever he needed to move about, had been placed in charge of maintaining order.

Guy and Will were standing apart from the others when they observed Toby Fraser being marched off in irons by two members of the watch carrying pikes. His interrogation had lasted the better portion of two hours. He was crestfallen and looked afraid.

'An outrage!' Guy complained. 'Surely Toby must have turned aside the foul accusation made against him?'

'I fear not. He has little enough wit at the best of times. I wager he could give no good account of himself. We are witnessing a terrible injustice, and are powerless to do anything about it.'

Guy seethed with frustration. 'When my father hears of this –'

'Of course! Father!'

Puzzled, Guy asked, 'What of my father?'

'Not yours, *mine.*'

'Have you, too, lost your wits? What light could your father throw on this matter?'

'None. But he might vest us with the power to do so. He has been Chief Alderman these six years past, remember. He owns property in Henley Street, and there is no finer wittawer in all of Avon. Why, he has even applied for the grant of a coat of arms. John Shakespeare is a man of substance hereabouts.'

'You *have* left your senses. What purpose in telling me what I already know?'

'My notion turns on what it is you do not know. Our attendance here is free, but my father gives money to help maintain the school. He is, I own, the single biggest donator of coin, bar the Church itself.'

'Your gist?'

'A word from his eldest son could end all that. Or at least Magister Armitage might be made to believe so. And with a free hand –'

'We could look into the matter ourselves!'

'Just so. I will go to Armitage this instant.'

'With me at your side.'

Will favoured his friend with a warm smile. 'Then we are of one mind. If Tobias Fraser is not the perpetrator of this heinous crime we shall bend our wills to prove it so.'

They were about to leave when John Dudley and Daniel Burrage arrived to delay them. The rowdy, Thomas Nashe, was not far behind.

'What think you of this tragedy, Will?' John said.

'Your word is well chosen. It is indeed a tragedy.'

All but Nashe nodded in sage agreement.

'And what would you do of it, Shakespeare?' he sneered. 'Write one of your tedious *poems* to put the world to rights? Hypocrites! I for one have no regrets at Gower's fate. The man was a brute.'

'It is said that it takes a swine to know a swine.'

'Save your cleverness. Can any of you in honesty say that you feel sorrow at his passing?' He thrust a chunky finger at John Dudley, making him flinch. 'Can you? After the way he beat and humiliated you? Or you, Burrage, thinking on Gower's belittling of your work?' He glared at Will and Guy. 'In your hearts you know I speak the truth.'

'Gower was severe, I grant you,' Will replied. 'But that does not warrant his death.'

'Does it not? I tell you, Toby Fletcher should be rewarded, not punished, for his deed.'

'You are a sad braggart, Tom, and your empty bravado is far bigger than your honour.'

For a fraction of a second, Guy felt sure Nashe would strike Will. Instead he barked, 'Have it your way, you snivelling weaklings!' Then he turned and strode away.

'Poor Tom,' Will said. 'All pisse and wind, signifying nothing.'

John and Daniel likewise drifted off.

Staring at Nashe's broad, departing back, Will added, 'This makes me think, friend Guy, that if Toby did not put an end to Gower it is not beyond reason that one of our own number did.'

Five and forty minutes past eleven of the clock ante meridiem.

'I can see you are bent on being vexatious, Shakespeare,' Armitage fumed. 'And a meddlesome... *child* is more baggage than we can carry at this time.'

Will straightened himself to his full height, a height above the norm for one of his age, and fixed Armitage with an unswerving gaze. Or at least what he hoped resembled one. 'I mean no disrespect, Magister. Can I take it that you will allow me to ask questions of the masters?'

'The threat you imply leaves me little option. For the remainder of this day, yes, you may pry. *If* the masters choose to speak to you. But you are on a hiding to nought. Fraser is guilty.'

'*Dum spiro spero*, Magister.'

'Then mark this, boy. Let not your thirst for story-weaving colour your vision. Nor your silvered tongue lead you into deep waters,' he added portentously.

'I am indebted, Magister.'

Armitage rose from his imposing desk. 'I have matters to attend to. I will pass the word that you have permission to ask your questions.'

He left the room.

Guy let out an audible sigh of relief. 'You took a risk.'

'I do it gladly to give Toby his chance of justice.'

'What now?'

'We inquire of Magister Webb the cause of his disputation with Gower.'

'Then make haste. We have but the confines of this single day. What remains of it.'

Guy exited. In following, Will's eye fell upon a portrait half hidden by the open door. He had rarely been in Armitage's private study, his *sanctum sanctorum*, and the dimly-lit picture was new to him. He lingered, squinting at the likeness and the inscription upon the bottom of its frame.

'Come!' Guy yelled.

Will shrugged and sped after him.

They found Nathan Webb in his own study, poring over the scriptures, as was fitting for one of his calling.

Having made apologies for the intrusion, Will got straight to the heart. 'Has Magister Armitage told you that I have his permission to ask questions of the masters, sir?'

'He did say something about you making inquiries on his behalf,' Webb answered vaguely. 'Is that so?'

Will and Guy realised that Webb, notorious for his vacancy, had misunderstood. He believed the boys were acting *for* Armitage, rather than independently.

'That is so,' Will confirmed.

Guy noticed that his friend had his fingers crossed behind his back.

'Then ask your questions,' invited Webb.

Will took a breath and plunged in. 'Shortly before Magister Gower's death, we saw you and he engaged in an altercation. Pray, what were you arguing about?'

Webb's thin smile froze. 'There is need for this?'

'Aye, sir,' Will insisted.

'Well, the bad humour that arose between us had to do with discipline. I took issue with him about the way he dealt out physical punishment in such a generous manner. It came to a head at that time because he had just struck a pupil for, I believed, insufficient reason.'

Will remembered the crying boy in the cloistered passageway.

'Of course, I agree that you students should be properly disciplined,' he added. 'Spare the rod, etcetera. But Gower was too harsh. We are a Christian institution. Love and compassion should govern our actions.'

'I understand,' Will told him.

'You can perhaps imagine how much I now regret remonstrating with Magister Gower so soon before the man's demise. God rest his soul.'

'So say us all,' Guy murmured.

'Is there more?' Webb asked.

'I, uhm, think not, sir,' Will said.

'Then you will excuse me if I return to my studies.'

They thanked him and left.

Outside, Guy brought up the subject of Will's deceit. 'God will forgive you, Will. You dissembled for a righteous cause. What think you of Magister Webb's explanation?'

'It is true we saw a crying boy, and I have no doubt Gower was responsible. And our Bible studies tutor is well known for his generosity of nature. Yet...'

'Yes?'

'All men's souls have corners where light does not intrude. We have only his word that the quarrel *was* about discipline.'

'You are wise beyond your years, Will. What shall we do now?'

'Time is short. My idea is that I go to talk with Magister Savage. Meantime, you mingle with the students and sniff out what you can.'

One of the clock post meridiem.

Will was agreeably surprised to find that the Philosophy master had no qualms about speaking with him on the subject of Gower's death. He suspected this was because he was Henry Savage's star pupil, and for the sake of their shared passion for Ovid.

Midway in their hitherto mundane conversation, an intriguing fact emerged.

'In due course,' Savage revealed, 'I fully expected to succeed him as second master here.'

'How so?'

'He let slip that he was preparing to return to his native Cumbria. To take up another teaching post, I presume.'

It crossed Will's mind that Savage's professed sorrow at Gower's demise barely hid his glee at the prospect of taking the dead man's position.

'Now your ambition has no barriers,' Will observed.

It was a step too far. A flash of malice lit Savage's eyes. 'I trust that your finger of suspicion does not point at *me*!'

'I merely –'

'Merely nothing! If you are so certain that the idiot Fraser was not responsible, there are others here with much more reason than I.'

'You would care to name such?'

'Kean, for one. He was constantly mocked by Gower as being an abomination in God's eyes because of that foreshortened leg of his.'

After that, Savage became reticent. Will made an excuse and departed.

He met with Guy in a corridor near the kitchens and recounted what had passed with Savage. For his part, Guy reported that his enquiries with the other boys yielded little not already known.

'Gower was unpopular, which we knew. More than one student openly confessed that they feel little regret at his passing.'

'It seems that there are fewer here *without* reason to detest the man than with it.'

'I confess myself confounded, Will. This rivals any plot you have written.'

'As yet, my friend, as yet. I was on my way to Ambroise Kean, in yonder provisions area. Accompany me.'

It took a little longer to draw out Kean than the others they had so far confronted. But in time he came to admit that Gower had indeed mocked his affliction. Will asked gently how he came by it.

'I served in a company with Fraser. We were both struck down in the same engagement, as unhappy Fate would have it. As Stratford men, and good Church-goers, we were offered positions here upon our discharge.'

Will didn't know about this connection between the men. Another piece was added to the puzzle in his mind.

'Tell me, master,' he ventured, 'doth thou think Fraser capable of a deed as foul as murder?'

Kean paused before replying. 'I cannot speak of another. Which of us would be so bold as to say they could see into the hearts of their fellow creatures?'

Will was about to pursue the subject when they were interrupted. Francis Quincey and the vicar of Holy Trinity church, Jeremiah Rowley, entered the room in a rush.

'You see?' Quincey exclaimed. 'I said something was afoot!'

The vicar moved forward. 'I am told that you boys have been troubling the masters and other pupils with probings into today's outrage. What game is this?'

'No game, Reverend,' Will returned. 'We believe an injustice is being done, and act with Magister Armitage's blessing.'

'That I did not know. What can you hope to achieve?'

'For start, whether the victim had enemies.'

A cynical laugh escaped Quincey's lips. 'It would be more pointed to inquire as to whether he had friends.'

'Would you count yourself amongst the latter?'

'If that were my lot I would hurl myself from yonder Copton Bridge.'

Quincey realised he had allowed the heat of the moment to draw him too deep. He tried to dampen the flames. 'Suffice it to say that we ploughed our separate furrows, Master Shakespeare.'

Will turned to vicar Rowley. 'Do you know of any enemies who might have gone to extremes to deal with Magister Gower, Reverend Father?'

'Am *I* to be put to the inquisition by a child now? As I understand it, the dying man uttered the name of his killer before he left this world.'

'It seemed so.'

'Then there is no more to be proven.'

'Perhaps not. Where were you when Captain Adams of the Watch sought you out earlier?'

'I am not obliged to explain my movements to a minor!'

'As I said, Magister Armitage –'

'May I remind you that I, as a representative of the Church, have dominion over this school *and* Armitage.'

'You are criticising the head teacher's actions?'

'No! I have known him since he came to Stratford from the north-west to take up his position. He is a fine man. And I have had enough of your offensive behaviour. You and your compatriot will withdraw at once. Do not doubt that I will consult Alderman Shakespeare about this disgraceful disrespect at first light tomorrow, if not sooner!'

Will and Guy withdrew.

They trudged back to the main schoolroom disconsolate and in silence. Once there, Will went to his heavy wooden desk.

'All have their reasons, it seems,' Guy remarked.

'Yet only one reason *enough*. But you are right, Guy. Any one of the masters, any of the boys, even vicar Rowley, could have committed this most heinous of sins.'

'Could we be wrong about Toby?'

'I still think not. But I am only a child, with a child's

understanding of adults, I confess. I would wish I knew more.'

'I say again, Will; you have wisdom beyond your years.'

Will sighed. 'This should be solvable. We are, after all, taught the principles of Logic. And something troubles me. It tickles at the back of my mind...'

He reached into his desk and hefted a tome.

Guy recognised it instantly. 'Ah, The Metamorphoses. Your beloved Ovid.'

'Aye, and the Good Book given me by my parents.' He produced the Geneva Bible. 'These are my strength, my comfort... my inspiration. I would be alone, my friend.'

Four of the clock post meridiem.

The *something* still nagged in the recesses of Will's consciousness. His hours of communion with the tracts he found so inspirational had not brought it forth.

He left the building, head down, and went to the others on the lawn.

'Our day is nearly done,' Guy said.

'Yes, and it closes dark indeed for Toby. We tried, we failed.'

They sat in gloomy contemplation of their defeat.

Tom Nashe arrived. Will felt, for the first time in his short life, that if the bully said anything to upset him he might offer another human being violence.

'Such long faces!' Nashe gibed. 'A poor brotherhood of the intellect we have here!'

'Brotherhood,' Will repeated, eyes glazing.

Guy was baffled. 'Hmmm?'

'Brotherhood... brotherhood. *Brotherhood!*' Will leapt to his feet, bounded to Nashe and pumped the startled ruffian's hand. 'Thank you, Tom, *thank you!* Your ignorance has opened a portal in my mind and let in a blaze of light.'

Nashe stared at him, slack-jawed.

'Guy,' Will said, 'I must away to Captain Adams. Be of good heart!'

They watched as Toby, smiling and tearful, was returned.

'*Now* will you tell us how you performed this miracle?' Guy pleaded.

'All pieces were before us,' Will pointed out. He used his fingers to count them off. 'First, the portrait of a man. Second, its inscription. Third, the chance reference to a north-westerly county. Last, and most shiningly obvious, Gower's dying word.'

'What of it?' Daniel said.

'Gower *was* naming his killer, but in his last moments he reverted to a classical form of expression. The word was not Fraser. It was *frater*.'

'Brother,' Guy translated.

'Precisely. The crime that took place here was that most terrible transgression of God's law, fratricide.'

'Look,' John said.

The Watch emerged with their new prisoner, and this time Justice was served.

As the pupils of Stratford Grammar looked on, Geoffrey Armitage was taken away in shame and chains.

'How did you know, Will?' Guy asked. 'Gower and Armitage did not remotely resemble each other.'

'No. Armitage favoured their mother in appearance. Gower took on the look of their late father, the man in the portrait in Gower's study.'

'And its inscription?'

'That noted an estate in Cumbria. Magister Savage spoke of Gower's intention to return to that region, and of how it was his native soil.'

'What motive could there be for so awful a deed?' Guy wondered.

'Gower was the elder sibling. He stood to inherit the substantial estates on the death of their father. That death took place a bare week ago. Armitage feared his brother coming into the family fortune. He knew him for what he was: a violent miscreant with a bent for the demon drink. The fortune would have been frittered. They had their last row this morning, and violence was the victor.'

'How came Gower to be here at all?'

'In order that his brother could keep an eye on him. Armitage, by the by, was the family name. Gower was their mother's maiden name. Geoffrey persuaded Samuel to take that name lest he, Geoffrey, be accused of nepotism. All this came out when Armitage was confronted by Captain Adams. He broke and confessed.'

'I do not understand,' Guy admitted, 'why Armitage sent us to find Gower, knowing him to be already dead.'

'Need drove him. It was Gower's turn to say break fast prayers, and *not* to have sent someone for him would have been suspicious in itself.'

'Well done, Will,' Daniel told him. 'You have sent a villain to the executioner's block.'

'I see Armitage as more tragic than black-hearted. Not unlike a character from an entertainment I have been pondering. Of which I have a few lines about my person.'

He reached into his tunic, brought out a parchment and cleared his throat. The boys stirred, a little uneasily.

'Of carnal, bloody, and unnatural acts;' Will read, 'Of accidental judgements, casual slaughters; Of deaths put on by cunning and forc'd cause...'

'That's enough!' they cried in unison.

'Go into trade, like your father,' Daniel suggested.

'Or the Watch!' Guy called out.

'Think again, Will,' young John advised. 'Methinks thou wilt never find your true path as a poet.'

Three Whimsies

The living are just the dead on holiday.
— Maurice Maeterlinck

Alternate Reality 1: Falling in Love

They were falling when they met, of course.

He was struck by how fetching her hair looked in the uprush. She thought the atmospheric pressure had made his nose attractively red and bulbous. They admired each other's muscular arms and spindly legs. She approved the huge lung capacity of his barrel chest. He found her watering eyes seductive.

It was him who made the first move, flapping to steer himself to her side and shouting above the roar in their ears, 'Fall here often?'

She laughed, lips and gums stretched back from her teeth by the wind, and called out, 'Is *that* old line the best you can do?'

Her gentle smile clinched it for him. His boyish grin won her heart.

After that, they fell everywhere together.

Plummeting joyously, hand in hand, their affection was plain for all other fallers to see. They shared private jokes, locked gazes, whispered and blushed a lot. They dropped in the company of mischievous youngsters, giggling at their somersaulting antics. They descended sedately beside elderly fallers, nodding sagely at their spillings of wisdom. Whooping and spiralling, wrapped in each other's arms, they dived with boisterous party folk. And when they kissed, the blood rushing to their heads rushed to their heads.

But soon their rapture was shattered.

They discovered that they came from rival families, warring clans who would rather die than be seen falling together. Their love could never be. But they knew they couldn't part.

He argued for telling all. She made clear the price of honesty, and said they were lucky not to have been discovered already. So they became furtive, resorting to isolated places where the unruly elements fell. Sometimes they met by the manna cascades, going down parallel to the flow that fed everyone. Other times their clandestine descent took place near the cataracts, the vast torrents of water on their endless journey from mysterious Up to unknowable Down.

It was near one of these that their secret was revealed. They were frolicking in the ambient spray, and had flipped onto their backs, his hand clasping her wrist, their mouths open to catch the slaking liquid. As they bathed in the fine, silvery goblets, someone glided into sight no more than half a dozen body lengths away. The figure disappeared almost instantly. But there was just enough time for her to recognise it as one of her male kin, and for him to have seen them.

The couple were even more circumspect after that. They couldn't stop themselves meeting, but their liaisons were anxious. Each passing faller was eyed with suspicion. Every sinking group left doubt in its trail. But when several days went by without incident they began to think they'd got away with it. That proved too hasty a judgement.

It happened at a funeral. The deceased was one of his distant relatives, someone he was fond of, and he felt an obligation to attend. She insisted on being with him, so they skulked at the back of the declining crowd. The departed was acclaimed, then the priest's eulogy turned to a peon of praise for the creator, the Great Tosser, who had instigated their descent, and who would eventually gather them all to His breast in the Time of the Transcendent Impact. With due solemnity, the Fallen was gently shoved into the Far Reaches, where the dead fell in perpetual grace. More than one mind dwelt, in that sombre moment, on the eternal verities of the human condition, rushing from who knows where to who knows what.

As they turned to soar away, he noticed them. A trio of brutes, drifting in their direction, icicle blades glistening in ham fists. Looking around, he saw most of the crowd had fallen off. He quickly got her behind him. The thugs zeroed in.

There was a flurry of kicking limbs, swinging punches, cracking head butts. He managed to dash aside a blade. It arced from his attacker's grasp, end over end, shimmering. He landed a blow to another assailant's stomach. The winded recipient tumbled out of the fray. He grabbed handfuls of the third man's hair and wrenched it. A tangled confusion ensued. Spinning, they glimpsed Above, shining white, then a flash of Below, shrouded in mist they never reached.

Next thing they were dropping clear of their scattering aggressors. He had a bloodied face; hers was going to show a sizeable bruise, and they were breathing hard. Nobody followed them, and as they gathered their wits they speculated that the men were relations, but whether his or hers was a moot point because both had so many.

After the incident, none of their relatives said anything or betrayed suspicions. Nevertheless they thought it best not to see each other for a while. That didn't last. Sure as Down was down, they were soon drawn together again. And now they lived in fear.

But there proved a limit to how long they could hide away, falling aimlessly, startled by every unexpected updraft. In the end, defiance outweighed trepidation. Slowly they returned to more populated falling places. Catastrophe didn't rain on them, and after a while they allowed themselves to relax a little.

They were almost back to what passed for normal when events came to an unexpected head. It was a particularly blustery day and they were hugging for warmth as they fell. Suddenly she cried out. Following her gaze, he saw her relative, the one they thought had spotted them by the cascades. But it wasn't just the appearance of this whiskery old individual that surprised them. It was also the three ruffians closing in on him with murderous intent. The same three that had attacked them before.

There was an instant of bewilderment. Why would they ambush their own? Perhaps they were *his* kith and not hers, as they'd assumed. But what benefit was there in setting about a puny looking, elderly faller? The old man started to yell. They ditched guessing and winged his way.

Taken unawares by the free-falling couple, one of the brigands caught a lashing foot in his face. Another found himself piggy-backed by an irate, pummelling female, while the third's jaw acted as her beau's anvil. The struggle went on for several minutes until, disproving the received wisdom that falling people mind their own business, others zoomed in to help subdue the bandits.

"As I live and plunge!" the victim exclaimed, in the fashion of aged patriarchs, as he recognised his rescuers. They steadied him, and all watched as the cursing reprobates were steered towards the Miscreants Drop Zone. It didn't take long to identify them. They were common rogues, related to neither family. In fact they belonged to yet another clan, notorious ne're-do-wells who fell out with everybody.

Her ancient relation proved to be a man not without influence, and in gratitude did much to heal the rift between their folk and her young sweetheart's. Indeed, in a display of human nature at its most pragmatic, it wasn't long before the formerly squabbling families forgot their differences and united against the scoundrels' clan.

For the young couple, life took on a brighter hue, and they decided it was time to settle as they settled. Their wedding was the social event of the season, and many members of both families dropped in for it. When the priest pronounced them man and wife '... for as long as you both shall fall...' there wasn't a dry eye in the ether. Congratulations ringing in their ears, they hurried off for their honeymoon beside the subside, their thoughts already on dropping sprogs. A new, golden future opened up before them.

And they fell happily ever after.

Alternate Reality 2: If You Can't Do It With the Lights On You Shouldn't Be Doing It At All

Chicory Hiccups went cyber after stabbing her pimp.

She didn't kill the little fucker, more's the pity, but had greatly lessened his chances of ever playing the harpsichord again. There was no doubt the rat deserved it, and the act gave her more satisfaction than anything else had in years. But the implications weren't slow dawning. Quickly stuffing a bag with a few essentials, ignoring his curses and threats as he sprawled in a pool of blood on the living room floor, she stayed just long enough to call an ambulance.

He wouldn't tell the police who did it, she was sure of that, but she knew she had to get out of the flat and away from her usual haunts unless she wanted to face his wrath. Home and income had vanished in a single moment of gratifying if ill-judged insanity.

It turned out to be the best thing she'd ever done.

Not that it seemed so at the time, trudging the moist streets with her possessions in a grip, blinking through rain-smeared mascara. Eventually she fetched up at Cherubim, a run-down coffee house where friends and colleagues on the game hung out, usually around the middle of the day when business was lean and their own pimps were sleeping or being bailed. While there, she had the good fortune to run into Myrtle and Zara.

It would be hard to find two more diverse people plying the same trade. Myrtle was gregarious, loud and not a little crude. If she was the last condom in the packet, she'd be the one with the hole. Nor was she overly blessed in the grey cell department, having once greatly baffled a posher client by referring to a new washing machine she'd heard advertised on Classic FM. According to Myrtle, it had a Wagner's rinse cycle. But she had the proverbial heart of gold; the kind of friend you met with over the phone to hate fat together.

Zara was the sort you wouldn't be surprised to hear calling herself a "cahl gal". She was all airs and graces. The type of woman who'd wear a shimmering ball gown if she were a guest on a radio programme; and if she ever deigned to do something as vulgar as eating crisps, it would be silently. Not that she was any brighter. Everybody remembered how, during a game of Scrabble, she defined Paraffin as the study of ghostly fish.

But for all their faults, they'd put Chicory right.

She was sobbing and moaning about her plight. What was she going to do? Where was she going to go? How could she show her face on the streets again, for fear of losing it? They surprised her by saying they'd dumped their pimps too, though neither as dramatically as she had. And they were doing well financially.

It was then that they suggested virtual sex. She was sceptical at first, knowing nothing about technical matters, but they persuaded her that not only was it her sole choice if she wanted off the streets, it was actually a step up in independence and income. The fact that they then offered to front the money for the deposit on a new flat for her, well away in a respectable neighbourhood, seemed to back what they were saying. Myrtle, for all her feistiness, and Zara, for all her cool, never seemed to have that kind of money in the past.

So they found her a place and introduced her to Dennis, an anorak who supplied the equipment she needed, set up her paysite and showed her the ropes. All on credit. It was him who suggested she adopt the Chicory Hiccups handle. (It referred to a particular oral speciality she was known to offer. Don't ask.) She swapped a pimp for a techie, but he was far too much of a div to give her any trouble. He certainly knew his stuff though.

There she was, new name, new drum, new *modus operandi*, up to her diaphragm in debt. About to embark on something they told her had no danger, no sharing with pimps, no risk of social diseases. So it was that, with no particularly high expectations and thinking the whole thing was a bit bonkers really, she took to Internet whoring.

She blessed the day.

All the punters needed was a net connection, a sensor suit and a credit card. She lounged at her end, suited-up, reading *Hello! Online* on another screen and faked ecstasy at the tricks' feeble thrusts. (She had considered Dennis' suggestion to have her moans and shrieks recorded, to be played down the line. But she thought that a little too hard on the johns, who were after all paying well for her services. She reckoned she owed them at least that much... authenticity.)

The money rolled in, she began paying off her dues, nobody hassled her. Even the phone bill wasn't a problem once Dennis did something devious with the line she didn't want to know about.

After about six months of this, things got unexpectedly complicated. Something happened that she had never known before, something she found both exhilarating and frightening.

She fell for one of her clients.

He didn't come to her via an ad or a search engine. She met him in a fetish chatroom where she sometimes touted. His handle was Xenon. Said it was a Greek word that meant mysterious stranger, which she thought a bit poncy. But there was something about his postings that had her returning time and again in the hope he'd be there. At last she suggested, in a private email, that he avail himself of her services. Oddly, she was almost disappointed when he readily agreed, but an appointment was set and his credit checked.

She didn't recognise him at first. Now he was calling himself Jumbo Grumpling. (The second part was a jokey reference to his dour temperament, though that wasn't a side of him she'd seen. The first part was to do with a certain physical attribute he claimed. Don't ask.) She thought that was poncy too, and daft, but held her tongue. To her amazement she actually enjoyed "sex" with him – she couldn't bring herself to think of it without the quotes – and they *talked*, which given her experience of men was a marvel. They even shared an enthusiasm for her favourite online multigender football team, AC/DC Milan.

In due course, as the sessions increased, she let him use a video link, so they could see each other while they were cyberscrewing. He was good looking; dark, muscular and brooding. She suspected he was married, which would be par for the course, and couldn't help but wonder why he needed to pay for it. But she pushed any doubts to the back of her mind, blinded by love, or its near equivalent.

Then, five or six weeks into their relationship, when she was considering breaking rule number one and suggesting a real world meeting with him, a bizarre event occurred.

It was late. She had just knocked off for the night (several times, in fact) and slipped out of the suit. Padding naked through her dimly lit apartment, she passed a full-length mirror in the bedroom. Something caught her eye. Something between her legs. A sort of glittery, twinkly glimmer that briefly suffused her private parts, then vanished. She stood blinking in front of that mirror for ages, but nothing else happened. Examining herself, she couldn't see anything amiss.

She put it down to an illusion, brought on by tiredness. Shortly after, the headaches started. They were low-key but persistent, and a couple of days later they were joined by itching. Not just down there. Everywhere. At the end of that first week she had another 'vision'. In the candlelit bathroom this time, stepping from the shower. She glimpsed herself in a mirror. For a second it looked as though a swarm of multi-coloured fireflies had nested in her bush. Squealing, she jumped back into the shower and lathered herself for another twenty minutes. When she came out again, timorously, everything seemed normal. But it shook her.

The following week it happened again, twice. One occasion had her transfixed for nearly ten minutes, staring at a mass of intensely glowing pinpricks swirling through her pubic hair. She grew seriously frightened.

Hesitantly, she mentioned it to Zara, Myrtle and a couple of the other girls down at the Cherubim. They teased her, generally made a sport of it and called her Floodlight Fanny. Her fears were mocked as groundless. Though from the corner of her eye Chicory thought she saw Myrtle adopting a worried expression between the laughter.

It got worse. Despite being someone used to dropping her knickers as a matter of course, many times a day, she became reluctant to do so. Then she started to glow through her underwear. It was time to see Dr Vulva.

That wasn't his real name, of course, just what the working girls called him. His real name was something unpronounceable in Polish, Slovakian, Croatian or some such, and he was old and a bit of a sod. The girls favoured him because he was discreet and up for anything if there was a bung in it. He hadn't seen the like of what she had to show him. It made him drop his torch, which in the event was superfluous anyway; she had a mini firework display on the go down there.

When the elderly quack straightened his creaking spine, he fell to pondering. Then he began mumbling about rumours and "other cases", though they were anecdotal as yet, and lots of stuff she couldn't follow on account of it being part foreign and part gibberish. When he mentioned DVD to her, she assumed he was talking about movies and thought him cracked. With a straight face he told her no, it had nothing to do with movies. Though the first D did stand for digital.

She was ushered out of the dingy surgery, undiagnosed and clutching a prescription for antibiotics, with a haste unseemly even by his standards. The pills didn't seem to help. To use Myrtle's terminology, her box continued to play up like it was radioactive.

It got to her sitting in front of a mirror and gazing at herself for hours on end, mesmerised by the eddying illumination in her secret parts, now not so secret. She became weaker, more apathetic, and neglected eating properly. The headaches were constant.

She didn't know what was happening to her. But whatever it was, she intuited it had something to do with Xenon/Jumbo Grumpling. If only because, shamefully, she'd allowed all her other clients to fall off, such was her fixation with him, and her condition had just got worse. She contacted him, told him what was going on and how frightened she was. He was defensive, and in turns sullen, angry, threatening. Finally she reached the rummage box of her vocabulary, resorted to damning his fucking bastard balls to fucking hell and burnt her bridges.

He changed his email address. She went into a decline.

Staying in bed all day became the norm. She'd draw the curtains and sit up naked, watching her sparkling nether regions like a child seeing its first thunderstorm.

Dennis, red faced, repossessed all the gear. The telephone line went dead. People stopped knocking on her door. She didn't care.

Now the brilliance shining from her took on a rhythmic throb, a pulse that echoed in her head and, soon, every fibre of her body. She was a cyclone of effulgence, pulsing energy like a heart on fire.

She managed to stand, a host to the beating, dazzling power of the virus flowing from her womb.

And surrendered to the light.

Alternate Reality 3: Good Brown, Charlie Grief

Charles Kummer had always regarded the human body as a near perfect consequence of evolution. But only near. To his mind, one thing marred an otherwise supreme creation. A shortcoming that spoiled its aesthetic. A design fault.

Bottoms.

A genteel upbringing allowed him to put it no more

graphically, and could have been why he found the arrangements Nature had settled on for waste disposal so distasteful. How could the likes of statesmen, poets, scribes, artists and spiritual leaders truly scale the heights, he argued, as long as this unpleasantness was part of their daily occasions? It was the great leveller, and it mocked dignity.

A 'scientific entrepreneur' rather than an actual scientist, Kummer had developed several inventions addressing the subject. These included the Kummerbum [TM], a snug-fitting body sash that hid the offending aperture. And his clockwork toilet duck and solar powered bidet proved a boon to the third world.

But such contrivances were cosmetic. Kummer longed to tackle what might be called the seat of the problem.

Once in a while, different branches of human endeavour merge and produce a whole grander than its parts, though it often takes a visionary to see the connections. In this case the dreamer was Charles Kummer, and the disciplines in question were Nanotechnology, Astronomy and Physics. Nanotechnology offered a general advance in miniaturised engineering. Astronomy and Physics came up with specific discoveries.

Astronomers using the Hubble telescope found the most distant solar system ever detected, in the constellation of Auriga. Radio spectrometry showed that the system had one planet very similar in size and composition to the Earth. This planet was designated BJT53548.

The breakthrough physicists made was even more remarkable. It came from a collaboration between two groups, one working on atomic particle research, the other theoreticians, surfing the outer reaches of mathematics. They came up with a device that could break down the molecular structure of matter, and via a beam, for want of a better word, instantly transport it seemingly limitless distances and reconstruct it upon arrival. This took a surprisingly small amount of energy; roughly the same needed to run a mobile phone. But the process had shortcomings. No life form higher than bacterial could survive the journey, and the payload was restricted to about a kilo, however much power was applied.

Scientists and the market puzzled on uses for the beam. Conveying small goods, sending explosives into enemy enclaves, delivering *really* fast food... It took the genius of Charles Kummer to see how this could be a blessing on Humankind. Private sources of development funds were sceptical at first, but Kummer's reputation loosened the purse strings.

The result was a pill. A tiny sugar-coated version of the matter transporter, which placed itself in range of the taker's bowels and bladder, and lodged there. After that, any accumulated solids and liquids were swiftly, painlessly spirited away. Frightful necessity had been abolished.

The crowning brilliance of Kummer's insight was where the refuse went. What could be better, and safer, than a remote planet orbiting an undistinguished star half a galaxy away? BJT53548 was to be Mankind's cesspit.

News of his brain-child caused a sensation. He was piled with honours. Everywhere he went, people feted him. Or at least the rich did. Because the pill was fabulously expensive, due to both its development costs and corporate greed. Kummer became incredibly rich himself as the great and the good clamoured to buy. Pills sold in bushels to captains of industry, executives of privatised utilities, bankers, stockbrokers, judges, military brass, archbishops and estate agents. While denying the pill to those who couldn't afford it, politicians took the gulp themselves. Patronising pundits, sanctimonious journalists and media barons made sure they got theirs. Well-heeled landed gentry who delighted in persecuting animals to death sought to place themselves above mere brutes by taking it. Crime bosses used the pills as treats for the favoured. Royal personages and peers of the realm, always knowing they ruled by divine right, aligned themselves with the angels.

Pills found their way into the guts of presidents, premiers, popes, ayatollahs, despots.

The frenzy spread to New Money, claiming supermodels and ageing rock stars. Trendy clubs, boasting their lack of toilets, opened for the pilled-up. There were envious pieces on youth TV. Geeks sniffed in Internet chatrooms. Kummer began work on a second-stage version of the pill, one whose transporter would dissolve in six months, obliging users to buy again. The prospect of further riches shone like a mole with a flashlight.

For the majority of the population, excluded, things weren't so bright. Fearing they were doomed to scatological inferiority, many became desperate. Life savings were withdrawn, houses sold, investments realised. Vast sums were spent on lottery tickets once pills were dangled as prizes. Bogus formulae appeared on the web. A black market mushroomed, offering purported clone pills with vulgarly exotic street names like *Shitkicker*, *Crapaway* and *Piss off!* These were always phoney, but it usually took a day or two before the buyers realised it. By which time the tricksters were away with enough money to pick up the real thing for themselves.

In admiration and envy, BJT53548 was soon universally termed The Dump.

Then a chance remark by Kummer on a TV chat show sparked another furore. Those taking the pill, he said, would probably be the first generation in an evolutionary process that would lead to the disappearance of the excretory orifice. It would heal up, but over aeons. Within days, a new kind of medical specialist appeared in their hundreds. For a lavish fee, cosmetico-proctologists would seal the fissure our species had borne since Adam. They promised a completely smooth and un-furrowed outcome. The wealthy jumped at it. In the common parlance of common people, the pill-takers became Butt Bungers.

Soon catwalks were awash with fashions revealing cleft-free buttocks. *Vogue's* Special Celebrity Derriere Issue was the biggest seller in the magazine's history. Venture capitalists waved goodbye to their back passages and loaned millions to dotcom companies devoted to the great blockage. The 15 year-olds running these companies blew the loot on pills, scalpel and thread. The pop song *A Crack in Space*, by Andrexia and the Puppies, topped the charts for weeks, vying for the number one spot with Pink Tissue's *Set the Controls in the Heart of Your Bum*.

The expression 'haves and have nots' took on a new, reversed meaning. Social divisions widened. Tensions rose when some of the privileged flaunted their good fortune via nasty outbreaks of upper class mooning. When the Bunged totalled about ten per cent of the world population, practical problems started to manifest for the Unbunged. Toilet paper manufacturers, bereft of the luxury end of the market, cut back on quality, adding to the plebs' misery with butt burn. Having less to cope with, sewage systems should have improved. But now there was nobody in authority interested enough to keep them properly maintained and they became a nuisance. Discreet signs boasting "We have no conveniences" were *de rigueur* in upmarket restaurants. Rest rooms disappeared from opera houses, gentlemen's clubs and practically everywhere in Knightsbridge.

But there were more insidious, psychological effects. Not least was a loss of confidence among the have nots (which is to say the haves), who could no longer nerve themselves against intimidating superiors by imagining their ablutions. The comforting thought that everybody had at least one function in common was tarnishing fast. Thus the Free Our Bowels Movement was born. There was unrest, and even riots. Unbunged militants adopted toilet rolls as their missiles of preference.

Discontent boiled on for a year. The stage two pill superseded the original and made even more money. Kummer swapped his knighthood for ennoblement. Bunged late comers weren't happy about having to pay continuously to keep the new status quo, but they swallowed it. They were more worried by spates of the unspeakable crime of transporter mugging. The humble went on grumbling, protesting, evacuating.

Just as a literal underclass was being established, another discovery was made.

NASA scientists found proof of extraterrestrial life. It was incontrovertible. For the first time, humans knew for certain that they weren't alone in the universe. There were aliens.

Unfortunately, they were on BJT53548.

Nobody had thought that The Dump harboured intelligent life. Or that its level of civilisation would be at least as advanced as ours. But no one doubted that after what had happened to them, the Dumpsters, as they were soon dubbed, were seriously pissed off.

Their displeasure expressed itself on a day later known euphemistically as Fragrant Friday. The form of their indignation was direct. Using a technology that homed in on the transporters of the Bunged, they simply returned the waste. All of it. In one go.

Suspicions about what politicians were full of were vividly confirmed that day. Royal palaces, legislative chambers and advertising agencies were instantly redecorated, with no option on the colour scheme. Dumpster returns materialised in the middle of dinner parties and tennis games. There were explosive, odoriferous spectacles in mansions and high courts, boardrooms and castles, golf clubs and wine bars. In the space of 17 minutes there was a worldwide cull of an entire stratum of Humanity.

Kummer himself went off with especial pungency at a conference in Stockholm.

Post the Big Burst, the Unbunged picked their way through the wasteland, handkerchiefs pressed to faces, and realised that the danger of giving people the opportunity to be like gods was that some of them would take it. But they also knew that Nature had a way of balancing itself.

So it was that the meek, the poor and the dispossessed inherited the Earth. And proved that you *could* run it without arseholes.

Polly Put the Mockers On

The row about banks moving out of the countryside took a new twist yesterday when the countryside moved into a bank.

Staff at the Ufton Paddesley branch of Clouts were taken aback when a customer wanted to cash a cheque. Nothing odd in that, you might think. Except this cheque was written on the side of a live pig.

Businessman Dirk Penhaligon proffered the pecuniary porker as his latest weapon in a long-standing dispute with the bank. 'Clouts have caused me a lot of inconvenience,' Mr Penhaligon, 41, insisted. 'Now they know how it feels.'

The entrepreneur, famed locally as a ballcock magnate, decided on his ploy after discovering that a cheque could be written on anything as long as it was signed and dated. 'I know my rights,' he said. 'It's the law.'

Clouts branch manager Sidney Doub, 59, commented, 'The rules clearly stipulate that we are obliged to honour a customer's request to withdraw their own money, whatever that request may be written on. For our purposes, this pig constitutes a cheque. Though we have yet to devise a humane way of stamping it.'

The "cheque", named Guinea by staff, is pictured here with twenty year-old teller Veronica Prancewinkle [on right].

Having pocketed his ten pounds, the amount the pig was made out for, Mr Penhaligon remained defiant. 'I believe I've struck a blow for many other dissatisfied bank customers all over this country,' he declared. 'They too should make their voices heard.'

But Sidney Doub ridiculed the threat. 'I'm sure I speak for the whole banking community in saying that our little difficulty with Mr Penhaligon is in no way reflected nationally. Bank customers are almost universally happy with our services, and have far too much good sense to involve themselves in these kind of antics. Believe me,' he laughed, 'this is a one-off.'

– The Qualmsley & Beagledale Chronicle

'Your mammals or your life!'

There was nobody else in the alley except the man blocking Eddie Markham's path. The man was massively built, and when a flash of lightning briefly illuminated his face it proved weathered, mean and desperate.

The gun he clutched had a muzzle like the mouth of a tunnel.

Sloshing through a puddle as he moved closer, the mugger repeated his demand with a hiss.

A chorus of muffled snorts and scufflings came from Markham's cart. Coolly, he stepped out of the reins. The would-be robber grinned, exposing broken teeth, savoring the prospect of enrichment.

'If you want it, you'll have to take it,' Markham told him.

The mugger's face dropped. Confusion clouded his bovine eyes. He glanced down at his fist. "But I've got a gun," he remembered. "I'll use it."

'Go on then.'

'What?'

'Shoot.'

'I *will*.'

'So what you waiting for?'

'I'm not mucking about, you know.' He raised the gun uncertainly, his hand shaking. 'Give me your livestock or I'll pop yer.'

'Go ahead.'

'But —'

'You going to talk or shoot?'

'Well, I —'

'You're going to talk, aren't you?' He made a show of directing his gaze at the automatic. 'Ah, I see why. Trying a bluff, eh?'

Incomprehension creased the big man's brow. 'A?'

'Threatening me with a duff shooter.'

'Duff?'

Markham gave him a knowing wink. 'It is as long as the safety's on.'

Ponderously, the brigand turned the gun side on and blinked stupidly at it. This gave Markham the chance he needed for a swift upward kick to the man's wrist. The gun went flying. Yelping, the mugger took a wild swing at him. Markham ducked and pummelled the thug's stomach. He doubled, expelling a loud *Ooofff!* Markham landed a cracking blow to his attacker's jaw. Imitating a felled oak, he went down.

Markham picked up the gun. There was no time to do the good citizen thing and get embroiled with cops. So he dropped the bullet clip through a drain grid. The gun he tossed into one of several large rubbish bins.

There was a rustling in the comatose mugger's grubby, voluminous overcoat. A couple of white mice shot out of it, followed by a small badger. Ill-gotten gains from some other poor devil, no doubt. The animals scooted off in different directions. Markham didn't bother chasing them, though he knew that if they weren't netted by somebody else they became treasure trove.

Ignoring the robber's groans, he went to the cart, lifted its lid and spent a moment soothing his change. Then he climbed back into the reins and continued his journey.

The rain was easing as he rejoined the teeming streets. Most people were hauling carts. Some were so big that their owners laboured to drag them, or else they were pulled by sweating couples. Others were small enough to bounce along on tiny wheels, drawn with a length of string. Markham's was somewhere in between, and about average.

As usual, the noises and smells were near intolerable. Slatted trucks nosed through the traffic, valuables bleating. Horns were honked at a small herd of Friesians being shepherded by nervous security guards. Naively, someone in the crowd pushed a battered supermarket trolley, their wealth on open show.

Markham passed a shop with trays of hamsters, tortoises and terrapins in the barred window. The standard offering for a jewellers. Next to it stood a block of luxury flats, and his destination.

A doorman checked his appointment, then directed him to the visitor's holding pens. Markham deposited the cart. Taking his ticket from a dour parking attendant, he jabbed his finger at him and said, 'Don't get any ideas. I know what's nesting in there.' He left the man suitably affronted and made for a lift.

He stepped out of it into an opulent penthouse apartment. There was no one about. He looked around at the sumptuous furniture and expensive ornamentation. But what really impressed him were the more obvious signs of wealth. A big tank of tropical fish, any one of which represented a month's income for him. On the marble hearth, a pure white Persian cat, eyeing them. And a gilded cage on a silver stand, housing a pair of lovebirds.

He moved to a window occupying the far wall. Below was a large back garden. It was surrounded by a high electrified fence and divided into corrals and wire-topped enclosures. Some held cattle, mostly rare breeds. There was a flock of flamingos, a group of antelope and a troop of baboons. He spotted llamas and camels. Craning his head, he saw what might have been kangaroos. He was obviously in a moneyed burgh.

'A gerbil for them, Mister Markham?'

He turned.

The voice belonged to a fat man. But it was self-confident fat. He was in his middle years, though his chubby, babyish face seemed unmarked by time, as is the way with rich fat. A pencil moustache slashed his upper lip, his eyes were powder blue. He was immaculately tailored. By comparison, Markham was a scarecrow in a body bag.

'Lonnie Fairfax,' the fat man explained, unnecessarily, 'at your service.' He oozed charm, but didn't offer his hand. 'You were admiring my depository?' He nodded at the window.

'Like they say, money chirps. If you've got it, flaunt it.'

'Good, we see eye to eye. How would you like something worth flaunting yourself?'

'I'd like it fine, Mister Fairfax. But I'm wondering why a guy who owns his own zoo needs a private investigator. You must have plenty of people on your payroll to do whatever it is you want doing.'

'To the point. I like that.' He indicated a table laden with food. 'Take some refreshment while I explain.'

It was an offer Markham would normally refuse, on the grounds of not mixing business with pleasure. But then he noticed meat, a rarity when only the rich could afford not to be vegetarians. He weakened.

'So how can I help you?' he asked, mouth full.

'It's a matter of some delicacy.'

Markham took a swig of wine. 'That's my specialty.'

'A matter I wish kept confidential even if you turn down the commission. Though I don't think you will.'

'Understood.'

'I want you to locate something.'

'Missing spouse? Stolen property? Runaway business part –'

'No, no. Nothing like that.' Fairfax leaned closer. His voice dropped to an undertone. 'Have you ever heard of... *the Macclesfield Macaw?*'

Whatever Markham expected the sealionaire to say, it wasn't that. 'Sure,' he replied casually. 'Everybody has. What about it?'

'I want it.'

'It's a myth. A story bankers tell their kids at bedtime.'

'No, Mister Markham, it's not a myth.' Fairfax's eyes burned with a messianic intensity. 'The Macaw is very real.'

'How do you know?'

'Believe me, it exists. It has narrowly eluded my grasp several times in the past. A bird of unusual size and markings. Quite a unique item.'

'I would have thought a man like you had enough already.'

'I have just about everything, true. But I don't have the bird.

Ergo, I must acquire it.'

'I bet you were a coin collector in the old days.'

It was meant as a jibe, but Fairfax looked mildly surprised. 'How did you guess?'

Markham figured that if a man wanted to throw his money away on a wild macaw chase he wasn't going to stop him. Particularly if the money was crawling in his direction. 'Okay, let's assume the bird does exist,' he said. 'How do I come into the picture?'

'I believe you may be able to obtain it for me. Based on information I'll supply.'

'You haven't told me why you can't use somebody who works for you.'

'You're not known to. That has its advantages.'

'I won't do anything illegal.'

Fairfax raised an eyebrow. 'Of course not. As to you fee –'

'I've got a set rate.'

That was waved aside. 'For this task I expect to pay well. I'm offering a Thompson gazelle as a retainer. And shall we say a fully grown African crocodile on successful completion?'

Markham was awed. The most he'd ever pulled in for one job before was a manky rhino. But he kept his face poker and pushed a bit. 'Expenses?'

'You think I have Labradors to burn?'

Glancing around, Markham came back with, 'Well... yes.'

'How about a brace of woodcock a day?'

'Done.' He raised his glass. 'What's the information you have on this bird's whereabouts?'

'I'm told it's currently in the possession of Ray Blythe.'

Markham choked on his drink.

'I see you've heard the name,' Fairfax reasoned.

'Who hasn't? He's one of the biggest crime bosses in town. Maybe *the* biggest. I can see why you're paying so well.'

'All you have to do is establish contact and negotiate the bird's purchase.'

'What if he ain't selling?'

'I'm prepared to go as high as a giraffe.'

Markham let out an appreciative whistle. 'You really want this bird, don't you?'

'Will you do it, Mister Markham? Will you achieve my ambition and bring me the Macclesfield Macaw?'

Draining his glass, Markham shrugged. 'I'll give it a shot.'

On the street he was approached by a beggar who told him he hadn't got two shrews to rub together, and could he spare a marsupial for a cup of coffee? Feeling generous, Markham tossed him a budgie.

Back in his shabby office, he'd hardly started telling his secretary all about it when she had to take a phone call.

'Markham Investigation Agency, Shirley Binch speaking. Oh, hello, Brenda. *My sister, Brenda,*' she mouthed at him.

'I gathered,' he mouthed back, and set to on a long thumb twiddling session.

Eventually she hung up, and gushed, 'It's her and Osbert's fourth wedding anniversary on Friday. I said I'd take care of the catering for their party. *And* I've been racking my brains for a suitable present. What's a fourth wedding anniversary?'

He was baffled. A not unfamiliar state in Shirley's presence. 'What do you mean, what is it?'

'You know, diamond, gold, silver...'

'Oh, right. Er, bubblewrap, isn't it?'

She gave him one of her blistering looks and changed the subject. 'What were you saying about this new job?'

'There's big bucks in it, Shirley.'

'You haven't accepted those darn pests for payment again, have you?'

'It was a figure of speech.'

'Well don't give me turns like that.'

He sighed. 'Just do something for me, will you? Turn up everything you can on Ray Blythe.'

'*The* Ray Blythe? The crook? You're not getting into something deep are you, Eddie?'

'That's why there's big... that's why the fee's high, if I earn it. But it's nothing dangerous.'

She looked doubtful but held her tongue. 'I'll get onto it.'

His attention was caught by the TV set silently flickering in a corner. It showed a race meeting from Kempton Park. He increased the volume.

Shirley spun her swivel chair. 'Do you have to have it so loud, Eddie?'

'*Sshhh*. It's the Jockey Handicap.'

The jockeys were in line. Several pawed the turf, straining at their bits. The starting prices popped up, showing the number of horses wagered on each runner. If his bet came in he stood to win a very nice string.

Then they were off. Legs pumping, elbows jabbing, the runners vied for lead position.

'Who's yours?' Shirley whispered.

'Number five,' he replied absently. 'Calls himself the Twelfth Primate.'

The jockeys were using their riding crops on themselves now. Their breeches were getting mud-splattered. Here and there, caps flew off.

'Come on, number five,' he muttered, clutching the edge of his desk, knuckles whitening. 'Come on, Twelfth Primate.'

His jockey was in the middle of the bunch, fighting to reach the front, jostling with the other competitors.

'Come *on*!' Markham yelled, waving a clenched fist. 'You can do it, boy!'

They rounded a bend and went into the home stretch.

'Come on! Move it! *Come on, Twelfth Primate!*'

The finishing line was in sight.

'Come on... Twelfth... Pri... mate...'

It came in twelfth.

He turned his betting slip into confetti.

'Lose much?' Shirley asked, unable to keep a note of disapproval out of her voice.

'I had a pony on it,' he told her glumly.

'I hope you're doing better with your more conventional investments.'

He punched Google on the remote. The Stock and Fowl Market prices came up. 'Hmm. Down a bit, actually.' He flicked off the set and grumbled, 'They should never have handed over the Exchange Rate Mechanism to the RSPCA.'

'That reminds me,' she said, 'I'm running short on petty cash.'

Markham went to the wire strongbox and fiddled with the combination. Scooping a handful of white mice, he deposited them on her desk as he made for the door, calling, 'Back later.'

He left her dropping the squeaking currency into a drawer.

The bar held the usual afternoon crowd of deadbeats and lounge lizards, although most of the latter were securely tethered.

Under his overcoat, Markham wore his best suit. Outside in the guarded parking lot his cart was crammed with wherewithal supplied by Lonnie Fairfax. The Dog and Ducat seemed like a good place to wait until Ray Blythe's casino opened.

Unfortunately, Markham hadn't reckoned on the attentions of a pub bore.

His name was George. For some strange reason he occupied the only table with a vacant seat.

George started by complaining about the cost of a pint, and how it had gone up from a canary to a seagull in all the local boozers. He grumbled that you could pay as much as a greyhound for a decent bottled draught, and went on to bemoan not having the kind of rare fauna needed to buy spirits. Then he hit his stride.

'That bloody Penhaligon,' he lamented, quickly adding, 'Pardon my French. But, I ask you, they call him an 'ero. Bleedin' *menace*, I say.' He sat back, arms folded across a swelling chest, and adopted the pose of public house oracle. Markham fought an urge to strike him. 'The banks were taking the mickey, granted,' he continued portentously, 'but can we really say we're any 'appier now?'

Markham shook his head in a vacant, noncommittal sort of way and daydreamed chainsaws.

'Anybody could 'ave told the banks other people would copy that twerp Penhaligon. So you had 'em taking in cheques written on cows, horses, sheep, all sorts.' He began jabbing the air with an uncertain finger. 'Where they went wrong, them banks, was in trying to discourage people by 'onouring 'em. Silly bleeders... 'scuse my –' He yawned cavernously. 'Took the cheques and gave animals in exchange, didn't they? A livestock cheque for twenty pounds equalled...' His forehead creased. 'What was it? A pair of goats, I think.'

Markham wanted to tell him that he knew his history as well as anybody. Or else bottle him. While he dithered, he was lost.

'But it didn't put 'em off, did it?' George ploughed on. 'Soon, everybody was cashing hedgehogs, tortoises and highland terriers. Pop stars were having their royalty cheques written on zebras. The banks had to do away with their vaults and build pens. Next thing you knew the shops were taking animals for goods.' He leaned in and confided indignantly, 'My boss started paying me in chickens.'

Markham wished he had a newspaper to hide behind.

But relief was at hand. Someone turned on the television above the bar. It carried a newsflash. There had been a daring robbery, caught on CCTV. They ran grainy black and white footage of hooded men rustling a herd of cows. A grim-looking announcer gave a telephone number and promised a reward that ran to fourteen hands. Then a financial wildlife programme came on and the sound was killed.

Fearing a further deluge of George, Markham avoided eye contact and reached for his glass. In the event, the pregnant silence was broken again when the jukebox started up. It belted out an old hit by the once fashionable Space Gals, a record that caught the spirit of the monetary revolution.

'Monkey can't buy everything it's true
But what it can't get
I'll find at the zoo.
Oh give me monkey
That's what I want...'

Markham checked his watch. Time to go. But something had been troubling him. He bent George's way and said, 'What's a fourth wedding anniversary?' Responding to the blank look he got, he elaborated. 'You know, twenty-five years or something is diamond and –'

'Oh, got yer. Me and me missus 'ad one of them. Let's see... fourth... fourth... Isn't that asbestos?'

Finishing his drink, Markham headed for the door.

At the bar, a young lad was paying for a round. Mindful of counterfeits, the landlord wouldn't accept the ferret he was offered without biting it first.

Ray Blythe's casino, Big Game, had the smell of affluence about it. Which is to say the smell of big game.

Having shown the doorman the colour of his magpies, Markham was ushered in to the plush interior. After a cocktail at the bar, costing an arm and a claw, he sauntered into the playing hall. He stood for a moment to watch the action at a roulette table, where a sun-tanned punter was playing red continuously, slapping down guinea pigs and occasionally having a hedgehog slide back as winnings. Bigger rollers were leading away muzzled cheetahs.

Wandering off, he passed a row of obsessives feeding slot machines with sparrows, and arrived at the blackjack table. He began playing, to establish his credentials, and managed to lose two salamanders and a gecko in twenty minutes. Then he figured it was time to see Ray Blythe.

He approached one of the goons in ill-fitting dinner jackets who watched the hall. Employing one-syllable words and sign language, he conveyed that he wanted to see the boss, on a matter that could benefit him. The lout took it in without dribbling, then told him to wait. Markham leaned on the bar, watching the bustle and half listening to the singer with the band.

'I'd like to get you on a slow goat to China...'

The goon returned, with a clone. They grunted for him to follow, and Markham wondered if they might be heading for a back alley. To his relief it proved to be a wood-panelled office big enough to have its own ecosystem, complete with the usual menagerie denoting conspicuous affluence.

Behind a desk fit for helicopter landings sat Ray Blythe.

That was a mistake; it only emphasised his titchy status. Three Blythes to one Fairfax, Markham estimated. And when he rose, his tiny frame was all the more apparent. Markham found himself bending his knees in an attempt not to appear to be looking down on him. It was a futile exercise. Blythe's head barely reached the PI's chest.

There were no pleasantries. 'I'm a busy man,' Blythe announced frostily. 'State your business, Mister Markham.'

'Fine by me. I only want a little... er, a few minutes of your time.' Blythe glared at him, ready to take offence. Markham took another step into the linguistic minefield. 'I mean, it's just a small... a *trifling* matter.'

'Not too trifling, I hope,' Blythe responded with a hint of menace, 'or I might think you were wasting my time.'

'The long and the short of it —'

Blythe's eyes narrowed.

Markham tried again. 'The... *gist* is that I'm here to make you an offer for... an item I think you have.'

'An item?'

'A certain avian asset,' Markham replied, adopting a conspiratorial air.

'A *what?*'

'A bird.'

'I've got flocks. What's special about this one?'

Markham suspected he was being toyed with, but carried on. 'It's a one-off. Very unusual markings. In size it's said to dwarf –' Blythe winced. ' uhm... it's big.'

'And would this... bird come from a northern nest?'

'It would.'

There was a tense moment while Blythe mulled things over. 'Just suppose I did know this commodity's whereabouts. What of it?'

'I represent somebody who wants to trade.'

'Who?'

'I'm supposed to keep that under wraps.'

'It's Lonnie Fairfax, isn't it?'

'Couldn't say.'

'You're a good bluffer, Markham, but it takes one to know one. It's Fairfax, isn't it?'

'Does it matter? The offer's genuine.'

'It's Fairfax. He's got the hots for the damn thing.'

'Whatever. Point is, my client wants to buy and he'll pay top beast.'

'If this bird's as rare as you say, why would anybody want to sell it?'

'It's unique, not easily passed.'

'Except by its lawful owner.'

Markham realised he'd implied Blythe wasn't. 'True,' he said slowly. 'But how much better for its owner, whoever that might be, to exchange it for less conspicuous stock.'

'There might be some benefit in that,' Blythe conceded shiftily. 'Leave your number and I'll see what I can do.'

Markham nodded, flipped a business card onto the aircraft carrier desk and made to leave. He stopped at the door. 'One last thing.'

'Yeah?'

'What's a fourth wedding anniversary? You know, gold, ivory...'

Blythe snapped his fingers at one of his aides.

'I think it's Latex, boss,' the goon opined.

Markham closed the door quietly behind him.

It was raining again as he stood in a doorway, talking on his mobile.

'... and I *still* can't find a decent catering company,' Shirley reported. 'As for a present –'

She took a breath and he jumped in. 'What did you find out about Blythe?'

'Oh. Er, more or less what you'd expect. Claims to be legit these days but nobody believes it. The police reckon he uses that casino of his as a sheep dip.'

'Money laundering, eh? Figures.'

'And he was recently suspected of involvement in a scam where polecats used to pay for costly shop items turned out to be low denomination squirrels in zipped suits.'

'Still up to his old tricks then.'

'You know what they say, Eddie: a leopard never changes his socks.'

'Do they?'

'Well, cold hands, warm kippers. Something like that. Mind you, that client of yours, Fairfax, doesn't seem much better.'

'Really?'

'Yeah, I checked. He was once charged with druggling smugs.'

'You mean smuggling drugs.'

'I know what I mean, Eddie. Smugs are small South American rodents. But you don't want to know what druggling is, take it from me.'

'I believe you.'

'Point is, both of them look like the sort of people who'd put ants in charity collection boxes.'

He glanced at the display on the phone. 'I've gotta go now, Shirley, my mice are running out.'

'Why don't you ever top it up, skinflint?'

''Cos I'm not made of wildebeest.'

He was cut off.

Turning up his collar, he got into the reins and began the haul home with plenty to think about.

Next morning his way to a meeting was blocked by a commotion on the streets. Riot squads were out trying to keep dogs and cats apart as bewildered older folk struggled to herd their income support. He'd forgotten it was pension day.

Eventually Markham got to the cafe and found his contact waiting for him.

He used to be known as Harry the Ferret. Since events made that superfluous, he was more often addressed as Erstwhile Harry. Or simply, if controversially, Harry.

As far as Markham knew, Harry had never been a boxer. But he looked as though he had. His not recently shaven head was shaped like a roughly hewn granite block. He sported cauliflower ears and a nose badly reset after a break. His piglet eyes were never still, and there was always an air of furtive paranoia about him. He hunched.

Nodding at his informant, Markham ordered a late breakfast. When it arrived he couldn't help but wonder why he was eating it. Early in the new order, people cottoned on to the idea of breeding money, and speculators with large quantities of rabbits watched their investment multiply to a fortune. That was outlawed, and certain species excluded from the currency. A normal birth, of a calf or lamb, say, was regarded as honestly earned interest and tagged as such. Rabbits, having no trading value, filled another niche.

God, Markham was sick of Bunnyburgers.

After a bite he dropped it back on the plate and got to business. 'I want to know what the word is on the street about a certain bird,' he whispered.

Harry's gaze darted nervously. 'What bird might that be?' he replied guardedly.

'Some say it's mythical. And it's from the North.'

'Would the thirteenth letter of the alphabet have some bearing on it?'

Frowning, Markham swiftly counted with his fingers, lips moving silently. 'Er... yes. Twice.'

Harry gave him a plotter's nod. 'What about it?'

'I believe it's in the hands of... let's say a prominent member of the *alternative economy*.'

'And would this wrong side of the tracks entrepreneur be associated with the second and eighteenth letters of the alphabet?'

'It's Ray Blythe, for goodness sake!' Markham hissed.

'If you know that, why ask me?'

'I want to confirm that he really has it. And if he does, where.'

'I might be able to help.' Harry's eyes skimmed the cafe again. 'For a consideration, of course.'

'Of course.' Markham glanced around the room too, then pushed a slumbering tawny owl across the plastic table top.

Harry quickly stuffed the bird inside his jacket. 'The gentleman you're referring to has a small farm just outside town.' He gave the location and added, 'If you were looking for something, that's probably where it would be. But don't expect no chimpanzees' tea party. The place is gonna be well guarded.'

'Thanks, Harry.'

'You didn't hear it from me. Right?'

'Right.' Markham stood, ready to leave. Then he paused. 'There's another piece of information you might have.'

Harry shrugged. 'Sure. A man's got to earn a crustacean.'

'You know how wedding anniversaries are associated with certain things? Coral, silver, that sort of stuff.'

'Hmmm.'

'What's a fourth?'

Harry creased his brow. 'I'll put out the word,' he promised.

'And you say you have a lead on the item's whereabouts?'

'Yes, Mister Fairfax.'

'But you're not going to say where.'

'Not on an open line. Sorry.'

'Your next move?'

'A reconnaissance. To try and make sure the third party really has it.'

'Very wise. Have a care, Mister Markham, and keep me informed.'

The line went dead. Eddie hung up.

From the other side of her desk, Shirley had displeasure written all over her face. 'Are you sure you know what you're doing? Ray Blythe's not the sort to tangle with lightly.'

'I'm not going to tangle with him, just take a look.'

'Your funeral.'

He was only half listening. Her PC screen showed stock prices on the Internet. He thought they were looking a bit heated.

Markham took a devious route, in case he was being followed.

An hour later he parked in a lay-by off a country lane and proceeded on foot, alert for guards. There seemed to be nobody about, so he eased himself over the two-bar fence surrounding the farmhouse. Approaching furtively, he noted that the doors were firmly closed and all the windows were shuttered.

A lorry appeared on the road, horn tooting. Markham dived behind a stone trough. Peeking over it, he watched as three men emerged from the farmhouse and opened the gates. They set to unloading a quantity of sacks bearing the logo of a bird seed company.

Once the cargo was dragged in and the truck had left, Markham crept from his hiding place. By the wall stood a row of dustbins. He went to them and began carefully lifting their lids. The first two were empty. But the third held several jumbo size

Frobisher's cuttlefish wrappers, and in the bottom of the bin he found a mass of millet husks, picked clean.

A distant, eerie noise froze him. Unless he was very much mistaken, it was a hearty squawk. Markham reckoned that clinched it.

He was halfway to the fence when shouts rang out. Looking back, he saw men spilling from the house. He ran, vaulting the fence, and made off down the lane. The cries followed, and he was fighting for breath when he reached the car and fumbled with his keys.

Pulling away as the first of his pursuers came into sight, waving their fists, he thanked goodness that dogs were too valuable to use these days.

Later, killing time while he waited for Blythe to get in touch, Markham took a walk and bought a sandwich.

He went by a cinema showing the new spaghetti western everybody was talking about, *A Fistful of Dormice*, then came to a TV shop with a small crowd outside gaping at the screens. About to investigate, he stopped when he noticed that his trousers appeared to be ringing. Fishing out his mobile, he took a frantic call from Shirley.

No sooner had he taken it in, and while he was still reeling, when somebody laid a hand on his shoulder. He looked up at the expensively-suited tough who had hold of him, then down a bit at the other two.

'You're coming with us,' the giant announced.

Markham dropped his sandwich as they bundled him into a stretch limo with smoked windows.

They wouldn't tell him where they were going. Wouldn't speak at all, in fact. So he spent the time trying to listen to the car radio they'd left on low volume.

'Less than eighteen months after Penhaligon presented his historic cheque, the UK went over to the Bulldog standard. Before long, Bulls and Bears on the Stock Exchange were trading in bulls and bears.' The goons

162

weren't paying any attention. Markham strained to hear. *The global implications were profound. Japan adopted the Goldfish standard, France the Snail and America the Eagle. Soon, every nation had based its currency on animal reserves. But now –'*

The driver snapped off the radio as the car swept into the underground garage of a swish tower block. Markham recognised it, and wasn't surprised.

Five minutes later he was hustled out of a private elevator for an audience with Lonnie Fairfax.

'You only had to call if you wanted a meet,' Markham told him.

'I needed to be sure you'd come,' Fairfax replied dryly.

'Now I wonder what you want to talk about. I don't think.'

'I had a brilliant idea. I thought, why pay you to negotiate the purchase of the Macaw now that you've found out where it's being hidden? It should be a simple matter for me to arrange its... liberation and cut out the middleman.'

'I'm sure that was never your plan from the outset,' Markham returned sarcastically.

'So all that now remains is for you to reveal the location.'

Markham started laughing.

'Bravado is very commendable, but it won't stop you telling.' He nodded at his henchmen. 'My colleagues can be very persuasive.'

But Markham carried on guffawing. 'You haven't been keeping in touch, have you, Fairfax?' he spluttered. 'None of it matters now.'

'What do you mean?'

Markham dabbed at his watering eyes and pointed to the TV. 'See for yourself.'

Scowling, Fairfax snatched up the remote. A news report flicked on.

'*... events came to a head. The international money markets have nose-dived. United Aardvarks has crashed. Konsolidated Koalas went down sixty points in the last fifteen minutes. Investors have withdrawn support from the*

Australian Roo and the Transylvanian Bat, and the European Cuckoo is under extreme pressure.' The newsreader was passed a sheet of paper. His expression grew sterner. *'There has been a run on the Swiss Poodle.'*

Ashen faced, Fairfax punched through the channels. All showed scenes of financial chaos. Mobs stormed the banks, making off with herds of antelope and flocks of ewes. There was a brief *vox pop* of a man sporting the apron, peaked cap and shovel that marked him out as an accountant. People were pushing wheelbarrows full of white mice into baker's shops.

'You're wiped out, Fairfax,' Markham smirked. 'You, me, *everybody.'*

Fairfax wasn't listening. Sweat sheened, he had two phones to his head at the same time as barking orders to his goons. Frenzy prevailed.

Nobody noticed, or didn't care, when Markham slipped away.

He braved anarchy in the streets. It was a little easier without the cart.

Shirley was in the office, but she wasn't alone. Ray Blythe and a cohort of heavies were waiting too.

The bantam sized crime boss moved closer. A couple of goons backed him. Markham braced himself for a duffing up, or worse.

Blythe loomed below him, his expression severe. 'It seems we have some unfinished business,' he intoned.

'Do we?' Markham responded in what he hoped was a casual manner but knew wasn't.

'Oh, yes.' Blythe lifted a well-manicured hand and snapped his fingers.

Markham flinched. There was an intake of breath from Shirley.

But no onslaught ensued. Instead, another tough entered, bearing a large wicker basket draped with a blanket.

'Looks as if we're all ruined now,' Blythe said. 'So I won't be needing this.' The blanket was whipped away, revealing the head and neck of a massive, disputatious looking bird with unusual markings. 'Give that to your boss.'

'I think Mister Fairfax has troubles of his own right now.'

Blythe smiled sardonically. 'Good.' Then he beckoned his entourage. The bird was set down and they all trooped out.

Shirley and Markham vied for biggest sighs of relief.

'Well, you kind of cracked the case,' she ventured, making the best of it. 'Pity the thing's worthless.'

'Bit of a drawback, isn't it? But we've got bigger fish to fry now. Probably literally.'

'So what are we going to do?'

'Have a party. Brenda and Osbert's do is still on, isn't it?'

'Well, yes, I suppose so. I mean, we might as well. Though I never did find a catering company. Or a present, come to that.'

'There's just one thing that's been bothering me.'

'About the case?'

'No, about your sister's wedding anniversary. You found out what a fourth is, right? What represents it.' A tone of desperation edged his voice. '*Tell* me!'

'What? Oh, that. No, I never did. Doesn't matter though, does it?'

He slumped, head in hands. A screech from the basket brought him out of it. He looked at the bird. The bird stared back, its beady, mean eye unwavering.

Markham hefted the basket and plonked it on Shirley's desk. The beast squawked belligerently. 'There you go, for Brenda and Osbert.'

'I hardly think devalued currency is appropriate as a present, Eddie,' she sniffed.

'Who said anything about a present? This is the catering.'

Juice

There had been a leakage of Joy.

'Siren?' Duthie asked hopefully, his finger hovering over the button.

Busy negotiating the van through rush hour traffic, Anders ground the gears and said nothing.

'Can we?' Duthie persisted. 'It *is* an emergency, isn't it?'

Anders glanced at his young trainee. 'Not a category one.' He cracked a smile. 'But go ahead.'

Duthie grinned back and jabbed the button. The siren began whooping. Red and amber lights flashed.

Anders put his foot on the accelerator. 'You've not been on one of these call-outs before, have you, Bob?'

'No. I'm really looking forward to it.'

'Don't get too excited. We'll be dealing with one of the more benign distillates, so it's fairly routine. But we still have to take precautions.'

'Against Joy?'

'Sure. In its way Joy can affect us just as much as the stronger essences. We'll need clear heads to get the job done.'

'So we have to wear the gear?'

"fraid so.'

'Not keen on that.'

'Like I said, this isn't a category one, so we'll probably get away with just the masks.'

'What about it being absorbed through our skin?'

'It'd have to be a hell of a leak to do that. And according to the reports this isn't that bad.'

'But bad enough to get us out.'

'It's what they pay us for.' He rounded a corner at speed.

The screech of tyres had pedestrians' heads turning.

'So what happens when we get there?'

'The main thing is to try to ignore any members of the public who've copped an overdose. The police and the paramedics deal with that. We concentrate on our job. Got it?'

Duthie nodded.

'I mean it about punters who might have been affected,' Anders stressed. 'If you've not seen a fracture before you might find it a bit… much.'

'I know what essences *do*.'

'You know what they do in properly controlled doses. A fracture's something else. So stick with me and do exactly what I tell you. Understood?'

'Understood, chief.'

Their destination was marked by an assembly of police cars and ambulances. A cordon had been set up around a squat, red brick building, and officers were trying to disperse a small crowd on the opposite side of the road.

Anders killed the siren and pulled up a short distance from the scene. While Duthie fished out the respirators and a toolbox, Anders flipped open the glove compartment and reached for an atmospheric hazard detector. A sniffer, as the operatives commonly referred to them. Then they put on their masks and left the van.

As they approached the cordon they saw that the police and ambulance crews were wearing masks too.

Anders checked the sniffer. 'Getting on for three times over normal.'

'That's high?' Duthie asked.

'High enough from this distance.'

They got a better look at the building. It was old, probably Victorian, and could originally have been a school, or perhaps a temperance hall. Above the double doors hung a scruffy banner reading New Dawn Evangelical Mission.

A policeman in an inspector's uniform met them. He wore

no cap, because of the mask, revealing a shock of unruly hair. When he spoke his voice was muffled. 'British Distillate?'

'Yeah. Craig Anders.' He flashed his ID and jabbed a thumb at his apprentice. 'Robert Duthie.'

The Inspector didn't bother introducing himself. 'I've got men tied up with this thing. Can we get a move on?'

'We're on it,' Anders told him. 'Have any of your people tried stopping it?'

'No. We thought it best left to your lot.'

'Right answer. Is the building clear?'

'It's okay for you to go in.'

'Good.' He took out his PDA and punched up the schematic. 'I need to check where the pipe-work is so we can —'

Something like a wail cut the air.

A middle-aged woman was coming towards them from the chapel's entrance. Her hair was dishevelled and her eyes were wild. She was waving her arms about and shouting, and there was a wide, beatific smile on her face.

'Halleluiah!' she cried. *'I have seen the light! I have heard the word and the word is good! Rejoice! Rejoice!'*

'Rapture OD,' Anders stated, unnecessarily.

Duthie looked dumbfounded, as far as could be seen through his respirator. The Inspector sighed loudly enough to be heard through his.

'Happiness is my lot!' the woman announced. *'My cup runneth —* oof!'

She went down under a pair of charging constables. The trio wrestled on the pavement, the woman still mouthing exaltations, her fixed smile intact. A paramedic arrived, and after a brief struggle managed to jab her buttock with a hypodermic. Whatever he pumped into her worked swiftly. She started to calm.

Anders gave the Inspector a sour look. 'What was that about it being all right to go in?'

'We've got *most* of them out. And you know they're not

dangerous, except perhaps to themselves.'

'They get in the way.'

The Inspector sighed again. 'I'll give you an escort.' He beckoned a heavily-built sergeant. 'Take these two inside and see they aren't molested.'

They left the Inspector and followed the Sergeant to the chapel's entrance.

'What part of the building do we want?' Duthie asked.

'Basement,' Anders said, consulting the PDA.

'There are other officers in there,' the masked Sergeant assured them. 'We'll get you through.'

A notice board stood beside the door. A square of card was pinned to it, on which someone had painstakingly written *I will see you again, and your heart shall rejoice, and your joy no man taketh from you.* John 16:22

'Afraid *we're* about to take it,' Anders remarked dryly.

They went inside. It occurred to him that if they weren't wearing the respirators this would be the sort of place that smelt of mildew and stale boiled cabbage. The joy itself, of course, was odourless.

The interior was ill-lit, with old brown lino and grubby cream and green paintwork adding to the gloom.

'This way.' The Sergeant headed for another set of doors.

They swung open before they got to them. A constable and a paramedic came through, flanking a manically grinning young man. Like the woman downed outside, he was in a feverish daze and voicing ecstasy. His legs were buckling, and he had to be half guided, half dragged. The constable rolled his eyes at the Sergeant as the trio staggered past.

The doors led to a hall. There was a podium at one end, with a lectern and a low table holding a large urn of flowers. An elderly man, sitting on the stage, was staring intently at the flowers. He wore the by now familiar blissful expression, but he wasn't raving. Joy's effect on him was mesmeric.

Facing the podium were rows of fold-up wooden chairs. A

few people were scattered amongst them, the remnants of a congregation. Some were as quiet as the old man on the stage, others noisily jubilant. Masked police officers and ambulance crews were trying to shift them. Several victims were being given oxygen.

Anders and Duthie trailed the Sergeant to the far end of the hall. As they walked, the afflicted called out, joyfully. A further door, slammed behind them, muted the sound. Two flights of grey concrete stairs took them to the basement.

While the Sergeant kept watch, Anders produced a flashlight and found the junction box. Once he got the cover off, the problem was obvious.

'See, Bob?' He directed the torch beam. 'Down at the bottom there. Corroded pipes. Put you hand in front of them. Go *on*.'

Gingerly, Duthie did as he was told.

'Feel it?' Anders said.

'Yeah. Like a cold draft. What do we do now?'

'We cut off the supply.' He dug a chunky, long-barrelled key from the toolbox and inserted it into the valve lock. With a grunt of effort, he turned it. 'There, it's done. This place should air out in an hour or two.'

'Do we repair the pipes?'

'No. We're trouble-shooters, remember. We stop the leak and assess the situation. Then the company sends in a crew to fix things and –' His mobile warbled. He slipped it from his pocket, hit a button and squinted at the message.

Duthie was curious. 'And?'

'Here we go again.'

They didn't use the siren on their way to the next job. Officially, it was more or less routine. But it had the potential to be dangerous.

'You're lucky,' Anders said.

'Am I?'

'Yeah. We're gonna be dealing with a restricted essence.'

'Which one?'

'Submission.'

'Wow. That's what the police and army use, right?'

'Sometimes.'

'So where we going?'

'Prison.'

'Prison?'

'HMP Forest Grange.'

'What's happening there?'

'The Governor thinks there might be a leak.'

'Major?'

'He's not even sure there is one. But some of the inmates have been acting a bit docile.'

'That's a *problem*?'

Forest Grange stood in what was once an outer suburb, now encircled by the city. Anders and Duthie expected a bleak nineteenth century pile. What they found was certainly grim, but it had all the hallmarks of the nineteen seventies.

They drove past high red brick walls topped with barbed wire until they reached a pair of towering, grey metal gates.

Once in, having shown their credentials several times, they were escorted to the governor's office by a flint-faced warden. They crunched along a cinder path, edged with white paint, that cut through skinhead-short grass. The prison itself looked like an East European office block, except somebody had installed windows that were far too small, and barred.

The governor's office was tidy to the point of anal. The governor was less particular about his own appearance. The elbows and knees of his suit were shiny. He had hair growing out of his ears as opposed to on his head, which was almost completely bald, and his blotchy skin was bathed in a perpetual flush. Anders thought he looked like a raspberry wearing steel-rimmed glasses.

'Frank Rotherton,' the governor announced brusquely by

way of introduction.

'What exactly's your problem, Mister Rotherton?' Anders asked.

'We think there might be an escape of Submission.'

'You're not certain?'

'Felons are devious. They're quite capable of putting on a front to get better treatment or a chance of parole.'

'How do you know that isn't what's happening now?'

'I don't. Except too many of them are behaving too... reasonably.'

'How long has this been going on?'

'A few days.'

'But you didn't call us before?'

'We weren't sure. Still aren't.'

Anders nodded and checked his PDA. 'I see that you've got Submission piped to just one part of the prison.'

'Yes, the high security wing. It's one of our contingencies in the event of an emergency, like riot gear and high-pressure hoses.'

'And you've not had to activate it recently?'

'Not for months.'

'Have you evacuated that wing?'

'Do you have any idea how overcrowded this prison is? How clogged they *all* are? Besides, that wing houses some of the worst offenders in the penal system and it's never been so quiet.'

'Legally, you're supposed to evacuate any area where there's a suspected leak.'

'You tell me where to put them.'

'Well, I'm required to report it to my superiors.' Anders started tapping on his PDA's keyboard.

'Be my guest,' the governor told him. 'And good luck with the Home Office.'

'Can we inspect the wing now?' Anders said.

'To do that I'd have to pull out nearly sixty of the hardest, most callous offenders you could imagine, with nowhere near as secure to put them. My staff don't relish the prospect.'

'What do you expect me to do? We've come to test for a leak. If you won't let us –'

'I'm not saying that. If I have to evacuate them, that's what I'll do. But I want to be sure first.'

'The best way to do that is to let us get in there and check.'

'I think there might be another way. Suppose I have one of the inmates brought out so you can say whether he's been exposed?'

'I'm a technician, Mister Rotherton, not a doctor.'

'But you've seen plenty of people affected by essences, haven't you? Surely you could tell.'

'Pipes, pumps, circuitry, yes. Those I understand. But –'

'Your supervisor, Miss…'

'Mason,' Anders prompted. 'Francine Mason. What about her?'

'She tells me you're quite capable of making the assessment.'

'Haven't you got medics here, or –'

'No one with your experience. And Miss Mason did say that British Distillate would be happy to cooperate, given the circumstances.'

Anders sighed. 'All right, I'll take a look.' He added, 'Is it safe?'

'Perfectly,' the governor assured him. 'The man I have in mind will be heavily guarded. He always is.'

'But if I think there's any chance he might have been affected –'

'Then I'll evacuate the block for you.'

Duthie cleared his throat, reminding the other two of his presence.

'Yes, Bob?' Anders said.

'How does this man normally act? I mean, how can you assess him if you don't know how he usually is?'

'Good question. Governor?'

'You're assuming the man in question consistently behaves in what you'd call a normal way.'

'Doesn't he?'

'I'm not alone in thinking he should be in a secure institution for the criminally insane.'

'This just gets better and better. Why *him*? Why not show me one of the others from that wing? Or are they all nuts?'

'Because he happens to be out of the wing at the moment, in the sickbay, and that's next door. I need this resolved quickly.'

'How long has he been out of the high security wing?'

'Not much longer than you've been here. The effects would still show after that short a time, wouldn't they?'

Anders nodded.

'And he's in the infirmary because he's giving blood,' Rotherton went on. 'So nothing to worry about there.'

'Giving blood? That doesn't sound like the man you're describing.'

'All the inmates with clean blood are given the opportunity to donate. I never thought he'd be one to agree. Come on, let's go. You can leave that here.' He gestured at the holdall containing their protective gear that Duthie had carried from the van.

They had to leave the building to get to the adjacent infirmary.

As they walked, Anders said, 'Do your warders have protective equipment? To deal with an essence leak, that is.'

'They use the masks they wear if we have to deploy teargas.'

'Hmm. Not ideal, but it should do for short periods.'

'It won't matter after today, will it? One way or the other.' He nodded at the robust door they were approaching. 'Here we are.'

They were taken to a small ward housing half a dozen beds, all empty. Three people were waiting for them; two guards and their prisoner.

Anders and Duthie didn't know what to expect. But the individual they were confronted with in no way matched any mental picture they might have had. He was short and slightly built. His nondescript features were mild and his hair was silvering. He looked feeble. If his grey prison dungarees had been swapped for an off-the-peg suit he could have passed for a middle-aged accountant with the Salvation Army.

When they entered, he tried to stand up. Not in an aggressive or threatening way, but rather in what seemed to be a show of politeness.

'Stay seated, Norman,' the governor told him.

The man complied meekly as the guards pushed him back into his chair.

'How are you today?' Rotherton asked.

'All the better for seeing you, sir.'

'Would you mind if these two gentlemen were present for a few minutes?'

'No, governor. Whatever you say, sir.' He gave Anders and Duthie a subservient glance.

They looked on as Rotherton asked a series of questions and his prisoner replied unctuously.

Before long they were back in the governor's office.

'I'm surprised neither of you seemed to recognise him,' he said. 'Still, it was a long time ago.'

'What was?' Anders wondered.

'He killed seven, that they knew of. The media had a feeding frenzy. Must have injured as many warders over the years, several seriously.'

Anders and Duthie exchanged a look.

'Yeah, well, I'm glad I didn't remember.'

'So what's your verdict, Mister Anders?'

Anders jabbed a thumb in the direction of the infirmary. 'That's as clear a case of Submission exposure as I've ever seen.'

'Ah. So you're definitely confirming it.'

'On the basis of the man we've just seen, yes. Now we need to get into that wing and find the fault. Then we can have a crew come down to fix it.'

'There's no other way?'

'What do you mean?'

'As I said, things have never been calmer on that wing. So...'

'Yes?'

'Couldn't we keep the leak going? Just for the time being?'

Anders stiffened. 'I'll pretend you didn't say that, Mister Rotherton. Prisons are one of the few places we pipe Submission, and its release is strictly controlled and monitored. You're asking me to break the law.'

'Not so much *break* it as... turn a blind eye. Just temporarily, to give us a breathing space.' He sighed, something he obviously did a lot. 'I can see from your expression that you're not keen.'

'You could put it that way. Now let's talk about the evacuation.'

It was growing dark before Anders and Duthie got away. The high security wing had been emptied, not without incident, and the fracture located. They left the repair crew mending it.

'Governor wasn't too happy, was he?' Duthie remarked.

'No.'

'But you can see his point of view, can't you?'

'Sure, and I feel for the poor bastard. But rules are rules. He should know that, of all people.'

They passed a multiplex. Crowds were queuing to buy tickets and inhale from facemasks in the lobby. The array of dispensers were labelled with signs denoting ROMANCE, HORROR, ACTION, COMEDY, SCIENCE FICTION and several other genres. The masks pumped out doses of Receptivity, each tailored to a particular film category. But they didn't cloud people's critical faculties. They enabled the viewer to see the intentions and artistry behind even the poorest efforts, so that comedy was funnier, adventure more intense, romance truly tear-jerking. Cine purists hated receptivity essences as much as they loathed 3-D.

'Doing anything special tonight, Bob?' Anders asked.

His assistant shrugged. 'Dunno.'

Traffic was heavier as they got near the centre of town. They slowed in a jam and crawled past a bar. Early drinkers were exiting. At the door a couple of bouncers manned cylinders of Sobriety, offering whiffs to the obviously inebriated as a lone policeman looked on. That was to make sure they were offering only Sobriety and not an intoxicating essence, which was available illicitly whatever the law said. A handful of customers hung back at the end of the line, prolonging their drunkenness for a few minutes longer.

'I think I know where I'll be going after we knock off,' Duthie amended.

He turned up bright and early for work next morning. Either he hadn't drunk to excess or the essence had purged the effects. It made no odds. Sobriety, like abstinence itself, didn't leave a hangover.

Their day started routinely. They were dispatched to a housing estate in one of the edgier neighbourhoods, in which certain distillates had been installed by court order. The Obedience, Sociability, Cooperation and Fellowship essences had gone some way to lifting the estate's reputation, but every so often somebody tried to cut off the supply. Anders and Duthie were there to check on reports of tampering.

By arrangement, a police van was parked in the estate's central courtyard, where the odd blade of grass struggled through compacted mud and discarded crisp packets. The pair of officers leaning against the side of the van, supposedly ready to help if needed, looked alternately bored and impatient. One of them toyed with his Pacification spray.

Anders and Duthie discovered that crude attempts had been made to interfere with the flow. They marked them, did the paperwork and booked a maintenance crew. Then Anders got a call and they moved on.

Their next job was at a shopping mall in a more salubrious part of town. A department store within the mall had Civility on tap in its staff areas, which the employees had agreed to, as required by legislation, although they did it reluctantly. Now the management wanted to pipe in Honesty, an even more contentious move. Anders' task was to assess the existing system to see whether new ducts could be incorporated, whatever he and Duthie thought about it. For a couple of hours they suffered hostile looks from the workers.

They were relieved when their next assignment came in.

'Though it could be tricky,' Anders reckoned, driving them out of the mall's car park.

'Tell me more,' Duthie said.

'We're going to a bank.'

'They've got a leak?'

'It's a bit more sensitive than that.'

'Meaning?'

'You know about bootleg distillates.'

'Course. Never come across any though.'

'How do you know? Haven't you ever wondered why a meal in a restaurant tasted so good? Or how great the music sounded at a concert? Didn't it ever occur to you that one of the unlicensed essences might have been involved?'

'I hadn't thought about it that way.'

'Well, it's rare but it happens, and the company takes it very seriously. So does the law.'

'That's why we're heading for this bank, right? They're using a bootleg essence.'

'They might be. There are suspicions, but nothing like proof.'

'Which one? Distillate, I mean.'

'Credulity.'

'A financial outfit wouldn't stoop that low, surely.'

'We're talking about *bankers*.'

'Oh. Right. Silly of me. But hasn't BD got a section dealing with this kind of stuff? Why are we going in?'

'We get jobs like this from time to time. We do the recee and if we find something we whistle up a security team. The cops and the lawyers can take care of it after that.'

'So *how* do we do it? I'm assuming we don't just walk in and ask.'

'Main thing is we stay only long enough to get the readings we need, 'cos we won't have the protective gear, obviously.' He smiled thinly. 'You get to play spies today, Bob.'

'Life's never dull with you, is it, Craig?'

'We have our moments. Get out a couple of sniffers and I'll show you how to set 'em.'

They parked several blocks away, switched their company tunics for off-duty jackets and walked to the bank.

'You sure these are going to work muffled under our coats like this?' Duthie said, patting the slight bulge his hazard detector made.

'They're very sensitive; they'll still register. So just act natural when we get in there and watch for my signal.'

The bank looked like a thousand others; a brick box, its windows plastered with posters of cheery cartoonish family groups embracing bags bearing £ signs. Interest rates figured large, followed by asterisks that corresponded to scarcely readable footnotes spelling out the reality.

They entered separately a minute or so apart, Anders going first. He made for one of the vacant ATM machines and took his time checking his account balance. Duthie went to the other end of the room, plucked a booklet about mortgages from a spinner and pretended to be interested by it.

There were a moderate number of customers present, most of them queuing. An ersatz wood door opened and a man in work clothes came out, followed by a suited official. They shook hands and the client left, stuffing a sheet of paper into his pocket and smiling, though not as broadly as the bank employee watching him go. Over the next five minutes the scene was repeated several times. Customers exited interview rooms accompanied by kowtowing clerks and went away grinning.

Anders signalled Duthie and they sauntered out. Back on the street they made for an adjoining car park.

'We set them for purple, remember,' Anders reminded his young aide. 'If that's the colour that shows, they've been using Credulity.'

Glancing about to be sure they weren't being seen, they got out the sniffers. Their displays showed lines, not unlike the mercury tube on a thermometer, and both of them were about twenty-five per cent purple.

'Feeling particularly gullible, Bob?'

Duthie considered it. 'Not sure.'

'Lend us a tenner 'til next week.'

'Sod off.'

'You're okay.' He slipped his meter back into his pocket, as did Duthie. 'Seems we didn't have enough exposure to be affected. I reckon they're releasing it in those interview rooms. Probably get the marks to wait in there for a while before a suit goes in with his sales pitch.'

'What do we do now?'

'Push off and report. Then we'll – *Shit.*'

'What's the matter?'

Anders nodded towards the street. A man of about his own age stood there, well dressed to the point of flashy and coloured with just a trace of fake tan. He had turned his head, saw them and stopped. He hesitated, perhaps wrestling with whether to carry on. After a few seconds he headed towards them.

'From the bank?' Duthie whispered.

'No, he's not one of them.'

'Do you know him?'

'Yes. Now button it and let me do the talking.'

The stranger reached them.

'Hello, Craig!' he boomed in forced heartiness, extending a hand.

Anders gave it a light, glancing slap. 'Fancy seeing you here, Jerry. Doing a bit of business locally?'

'Yeah.'

'In that bank, perhaps?'

'Bank?' He looked at the building in question, registering surprise at its existence. 'No, not there. Further up the high street.' He waved vaguely in the direction he had come from. Then he seemed to notice Duthie for the first time, or made out that he had. 'Who's this then? New boy, is it? Little helper for you?'

Duthie's polite smile began to resemble rigor mortis.

'Robert Duthie,' Anders said, 'my assistant. Bob, this is Jerry.'

'Jerry Grogan,' the other filled in, 'Essential Essences PLC. Here, have my card.' He thrust it at Duthie and instantly lost interest in him. 'So, still with the old firm are you, Craig?'

'Still there.'

'Been a long time. Ever think of making a change?'

'Not really.'

'Plenty of opportunities out in the big bad world, you know. At Essential, for instance. Very go ahead company, building a nice customer base. Always room there for somebody with experience like yourself.'

'I don't think so, Jerry. I'm happy where I am.'

'Pity. Still, the boy's got my card if you should ever –'

'Right.'

An awkward silence descended.

'Well,' Anders said at last, 'we've got to push on.'

'Course,' Grogan replied. He looked relieved. 'We really ought to get together for that drink some time.'

Anders didn't say anything.

Grogan made a pistol gesture with his hand and pointed at Duthie. 'Mind how you go, kid. Don't let him work you to death. See ya, Craig.'

'Yeah, see you.'

Grogan went back to the street and was soon out of sight.

'You were cold as a witch's tit to him,' Duthie remarked.

'He only spoke to us because he couldn't avoid it. Did you notice that?'

'Yeah, and granted he was a bit of a git, but —'

'He used to work at BD. We started there together, in fact. He left under a cloud a few years back. Bounced around the trade a bit and wound up with Essential.'

'Who I've never heard of.' Duthie was staring at the card.

'One of the independents. On the fringe of the business, if you know what I mean.'

'You said he left BD under a cloud.'

'They weren't able to prove anything. But they knew he was bent. We all did.'

'How can you fiddle in this job?'

'Lots of ways.' He counted off on his fingers. 'Bypassing the system and connecting people for backhanders, messing around with the billing, falsifying the records so customers were listed as having a different, less powerful essence than the one they were actually being supplied with, contrary to their licence. It got to the point where he was suspected of outright theft. Canisters were going missing from the depots. It all came to a head when a brothel got raided and the police found the place had been illegally piped up for Joy. It's not *funny*, Bob. These distillates are tightly controlled for a reason. Some of them are dangerous.'

Duthie wiped the grin off his face. 'Sorry, chief.'

'The question is, what was Grogan doing here today, of all places?'

'Do you think he maybe —'

Anders' phone rang. He excused himself and answered it. The conversation was brief and one-sided, with Anders doing most of the listening.

'The boss,' he explained when he hung up.

'Another job?'

'No. We're wanted at head office. Pronto.'

Befitting its status as the biggest, longest-established company in the industry, British Distillate's headquarters were imposing and brash.

Even before they finished parking, Anders realised he had been summoned to something special. He recognised plenty of familiar faces among the other people arriving.

Duthie did, too. 'Lot of our fellow inspectors here.'

'Looks like all of them.'

'Does this happen very often?'

'Hardly ever. Come on, let's find out what's got Francine's knickers in a twist.'

There must have been fifty or sixty people in the cafeteria, one of the HQ's largest spaces. Virtually every field operative from Anders' department was there, exchanging greetings, trading speculations. Anders and Duthie found seats near the back.

The racket died down when Francine Mason came in. She was not young, but young for the position she held. Grown a little plump, and slightly shorter than the norm, she power-dressed and wore her dark hair long. If Executive Director Mason were a stick of rock she'd have *Company* running right through her.

She mounted a low dais on one side of the room. When she spoke, nobody had trouble hearing her. 'Thank you all for coming. I'll try not to take too long. The authorities, and the company, believe that there's a new source of illegal distillates. We've seen a steep increase in unlicensed and even forbidden essences in the last few months. Typically it's clandestine piping-up. But the police have been seizing a worrying number of distillates in canisters, including some of the most dangerous. And of course now that the underworld's worked out how to manufacture distillates, we don't even know if the stuff they're peddling is properly formulated. So it's doubly risky.'

Somebody stuck their hand in the air and she nodded to him.

'Any idea who's doing it?' Anders knew the man only by

name.

'We've got various leads,' Mason told him. 'But whoever it is doesn't seem too choosey about who they sell to or who they steal from. We've had cases recently where consignments of Courage intended for the military were diverted to street gangs. There's also been the disappearance of a shipment of Hope donated for charitable work overseas, and an incident with bootleg Gluttony that...' She made a face. 'Well, let's just say it ended unhappily. So this situation is our priority at the moment. I'm going to farm out as many of your routine calls as I can to back-up crews. They're not as highly trained or as experienced as you, but –' There was a rumble of protest. 'Under the circumstances,' she assured them, 'the union are okay with that, and I promise we'll have you back to normal as soon as we get this thing cracked.' That quietened them. 'Meantime, I want you concentrating on call-outs that might have some bearing on the bootleggers. You'll be briefed before you leave today, and given new assignment sheets. Just stay seated and we'll get through it as quickly as we can. Thank you.'

A forest of arms went up and she began briskly fielding questions.

'It really never is dull round here, is it?' Duthie said.

'I think we could do without this kind of excitement.'

'Oh, don't be such a stick in the mud, Craig. Don't you ever long for a bit of adrenalin?'

'Not as much as you obviously do. I'd prefer to get on with the job we're supposed to be doing rather than playing at cops and robbers.'

'You reckon it could be risky then?'

'Could be. Though we'll be expected just to take readings, check connections, that kind of stuff. Anything needed beyond that, we speed dial the police.'

'Pity. A bit of action might brighten things up.'

'The recklessness of youth.'

'I'll have you know that I'm –'

'Hang on, here comes Francine.'

She gave them a fleeting smile as she sat. 'Craig. Robert.'

'Francine,' Anders returned.

Duthie seemed a mite overawed and just nodded.

Mason wasted no more time on niceties. 'I think that visit you made to the bank today might have some bearing on all this.'

'So do I,' Anders replied. 'There was something I didn't mention in my report. After we came out we bumped into Jerry Grogan.'

'*Grogan?* Interesting.'

'You said it.'

'He was at the bank?'

'Not far from it.'

'Doesn't mean he was involved.'

'No, but –'

'We have to tread carefully, Craig. Whatever Grogan's reputation, Essential's an accredited company. We can't go throwing mud without proof.'

'I'd say Grogan being in the area's all the proof you need.'

'You know it's not. But I'll pass what you've told me to the appropriate authorities.' She sighed, and her tone softened. 'I'm not saying I don't think there's something in it, Craig, but we're operating in a different world since the government in its wisdom loosened the regulations on this industry. We had it good for a long time. The so called big four, that is: the Divine Corporation, Quintessence, Chi, and us. Now we've got a swarm of independents like Essential nibbling at the edges.'

'What do we know about Essential?'

'Not much. They're small, basically a niche supplier. Sharp operators. Our sales people certainly aren't among their fans. But as far as we can tell, they're clean.'

'It doesn't mean their employees aren't freelancing on the side, the way Grogan was here.'

'We don't know that. And frankly I'm more concerned about unregistered criminal outfits selling anything to anybody.

Can you imagine what terrorists could do with some of the distillates if they got hold of them? Doesn't bear thinking about. But we're not going to sort things out sitting here.' She took a sheet of paper from the folder she was holding and handed it to him. 'Your assignment.'

Anders glanced at it and seemed impressed. 'Unusual.'

'Very, and completely prohibited. I don't have to tell you how hazardous this one could be. So take care. Just assess and report, OK? And if things get choppy pull out and let the police take the strain.'

'Got it.'

'Come on then, out with it,' Duthie urged. 'What's the job?'

They were heading for the centre of town. Rush hour was nearing and traffic was building up, but Anders resisted the urge to switch on the siren.

'We're going to be looking for one of the rarest distillates,' he said. 'Luck.'

'You're kidding me! Luck? I thought that was just an urban myth.'

'No, it's real. But it's kept under tight wraps and seldom used officially.'

'Officially?'

'I've heard rumours about diplomats breathing it before tricky negotiations with foreign governments, and special forces using it on hard missions. I'd guess the intelligence services are fond of it. Other than those kind of things, if they really happen, Luck's strictly forbidden.'

'But now it's being used.'

'Maybe. But it'd have to be incredibly expensive, something only the very wealthy could afford.'

'People who've had enough luck already.'

'Yeah. And there's a lot of grumbling about the widening gap between the rich and poor as it is. If this stuff's starting to circulate we could see that getting much worse. It should be called Good Luck, by the way, 'cos nobody's going to want the bad kind. But if it's poorly made, who knows? Maybe it'd be *un*fortunate. That's another problem.'

Duthie soaked that in for a moment, then asked, 'So where're we going?'

'Parker's. The casino.'

'What would they want Luck for? They like their punters to be *unlucky*, don't they?'

'I reckon they'd use it to let the gamblers win a couple of times. That tempts them to stake more. But they don't get exposed to Luck when they come to lay the big bets, so they go back to the usual odds.'

'Which means the house wins. Why doesn't the casino just rig their wheels?'

'It's not all roulette, for a start. Buying a banned distillate's easier and they don't risk their licenses.'

They rode on without saying too much more. The main thoroughfares were clogging, so Anders took to the back doubles where traffic was lighter.

'How much further?' Duthie asked.

'Nearly there.'

They stopped at a set of lights. At the same time an unmarked truck approaching from the opposite direction also came to a halt. It was open-backed, with its load covered by a tarpaulin. The truck's windscreen was grubby, but it was just possible to make out who the driver was.

'Isn't that Jerry Grogan?' Duthie said.

'You're right, it is. And he's seen us.'

The lights changed and the truck surged forward, turned sharply, cut across the line of oncoming traffic and took a right. Anders revved, crunched gears and went after him, ignoring the angry hoots of braking motorists.

Duthie was shaken. 'What you doing? What about the job?'

'He's coming from where we're going. Bit of a coincidence, don't you think?'

'He's picking up speed. What do you reckon he's got in there?'

'Nothing he wants to get caught with, the rate he's going.'

There were fewer vehicles on the street they were travelling along, so Anders put his foot down. Ahead, Grogan shot over a junction.

'He just went through a red light!' Duthie exclaimed. 'Shouldn't we call this in, Craig?'

'In a minute. Let's see where he's going.'

Duthie thought Anders was going to run the light, just like Grogan had, and gripped the dashboard, knuckles whitening. But it flicked to amber a second before they got there and they sailed across.

Anders hit the siren button. The throbbing crimson and orange warning lights reflected on their bonnet.

'Can we do that? We're not the cops.'

'If he's got something he shouldn't have in that load we're justified, Bob.'

Grogan took an abrupt left without indicating. Anders managed to follow. The street they entered was run-down. Grimy terraced houses stood alongside deserted light industrial workshops and roofless warehouses. The truck put on a further burst of speed.

Then Grogan tried for another last minute turn, to the right this time. The turn was acute and the truck's velocity was high. Its left-side wheels came off the ground. For a split second it looked as though it might just manage the bend. But the angle was too much. The lorry tilted and its load shifted. Control was lost. The truck hit the kerb and flipped onto its back with a tremendous crash. Its cargo of cylinders scattered in all directions.

Anders stamped on the brakes. The van skidded to a halt a block to the rear of the wreck.

Duthie cried *Jesus Christ!'* Ripping off his seat belt he got the door open and leapt out.

'No!' Anders yelled. 'Stay here! It's dangerous!'

The youth ignored him and dashed towards the truck.

Anders groped for his mask and slipped it on. Grabbing another for Duthie, he scrambled out of the van and headed for the wreck.

A stiff wind was blowing, churning litter and brown leaves.

Duthie was at the truck, crouching to stare into the upturned cab. A couple of the vehicle's wheels were still spinning and smoke was rising from it. Afraid it was going to explode, Anders began to run, cursing himself for being so out of shape.

He saw Duthie back off from the wreckage, then turn and run away in the opposite direction. Baffled, and in shock, Anders shouted, frustrated that the mask muted the sound.

Breathing hard, he reached the scene. Bits of the broken windscreen crunched under his feet. Scores of canisters were strewn across the road and pavements. Many of them were fractured.

He knelt and gazed into the cab. Grogan was still strapped in, hanging limply like a puppet, covered in blood. He looked badly injured. Possibly dead.

There was a din of breaking glass from along the road. And again. He saw Duthie kicking in shop windows as he moved farther away. Anders resisted the urge to lift his mask and call to him. Reaching for his mobile, he swore when he realised he'd left it in the van. He decided to try getting Grogan out.

As he stooped again his eye was caught by fragments of a shattered cylinder. One piece had the letters *NA* on it, stencilled in white; presumably part of the name of the distillate it held. Or had held. Another read *RCHY*. He struggled to open the truck's door. Its frame was twisted and he couldn't budge it. He was considering whether to go back to the van for the phone and his tool kit when he heard more glass breaking. Not just from where Duthie had gone but from several different directions.

He straightened and listened. Car horns were sounding. Shouts and screams were coming from all sides. He saw what looked like a crowd gathering outside a building way down the road, and although he couldn't be sure he thought there were flames issuing from it.

Feeling a chill that had nothing to do with the weather he was again aware of the wind.

He trod on another jagged shard of canister. As he kicked it aside he noticed that it was marked with the letter *A*.

Anders heard distant sirens, and what could have been gunfire.

The Gripes of Wrath

The migraine started as soon as he read what *The Times* had to say about *Born and Bled*.

Following a lengthy and vicious dissection of the novel, the critic, Philip Bradshaw, ended with: *'It's nearly twenty years since Ivor Drummond took the crime genre by storm with* I Left My Gat in San Francisco, *his first novel. He honed his skills with subsequent books.* Proof Positive *dealt with murders in a blood bank;* My Learned Fiend *centred on a psychopathic barrister;* Cross My Palm With Caution *depicted fraudulent psychics on a killing spree, and* You're a Long Time Dead *featured a homicidal undertaker. These and others in Drummond's canon established him as one of the most popular, and quirky, commercial authors of the last two decades. But readers of his current offering will be asking what went wrong. Indeed, they may have been asking that very question for some time, as cracks in the façade began to appear with his two previous books,* Acid Reign *and* You May Kiss the Bribe. *But whereas those titles were merely flawed,* Born and Bled *is positively broken-backed.*

To the discerning reader the decline of an author once so innovative must be a cause for regret. But the reality is that barrel-scraping is never a dignified pastime, and to subject the public to this shallow, lacklustre and ultimately inconsequential fare is little short of contemptuous. It's sad to see a writer grow mentally fat and complacent, and throwing trash into the faces of loyal readers for the sake of another pay day. The abiding impression of Mr Drummond is akin to an old horse plodding, not into the rosy sunset of an illustrious career, but toward the gates of the knackers' yard.'

Drummond wasn't prone to migraines, but getting one seemed understandable in the circumstances. This was, after all, the first review. He was apprehensive about those to follow.

Ivor Drummond was what people used to call well preserved. He still had all his hair, a dark mop of it, unaided by dye. For vanity's sake he had adopted contact lenses a decade ago. A comfortable income, that great aid to looking younger, meant his tan was real and his gym membership paid-up. He was reasonably fit, for a writer.

The migraine, headache, whatever it was, made it hard for him to think. He took a couple of Veganin, washed down with a large whiskey, and went back to bed. But not back to sleep. Pain and resentment tormented him. After several hours the former subsided. The latter grew, mutating into anger. Its focus was Philip Bradshaw.

Throwing aside the bedclothes, he padded to his workroom and fired up the desktop. He usually approached his blog with little enthusiasm, regarding all so called social media as a drain on his time and creativity, while reluctantly accepting such things were expected of authors these days. Now he saw a use for it.

He wrote a rebuttal. Quoting extensively from Bradshaw's review, he countered every point. He argued against the validity of the criticism, along with Bradshaw's reasoning and his qualifications for passing judgement. He referred to Shaw's epigram about critics being to writers what dogs are to lampposts, and even mocked Bradshaw's grammar. Seized by the kind of passion he was only used to when writing fiction, he let rip with a litany of colourful abuse that questioned everything from his victim's competence to his paternity.

The piece finished: *Philip Bradshaw is pleased to picture me as an ageing nag fit only for cat food. If allowed a similar flight of fancy, I'm happy to imagine him falling prey to some event that stills his hand and renders him incapable of churning out the drivel he dishonestly claims as literary criticism. An occurrence I'm sure the reading public would greet with relief, if not actual jubilation.'*

Drummond gave what he'd written a quick once-over, then hit the *Post* button.

At around ten the next morning he got a call from Clarrie Lambert.

'That blog was a mistake,' she said.

'I'm flattered that you read it.'

'I'm serious. You've been round the block a few times, Ivor; you know how these things work.'

'Drummond mugged me. Why shouldn't I bite back?'

'Because it'll get messy, and it makes you look like you can't take a little criticism.'

'*A little criticism?* It was Pearl Harbour! A shit storm.'

'And you'll piss off the other critics. They hunt in packs, you know.'

'Well, it made me feel better.'

'In future think about maintaining a dignified silence.'

'In future? I should expect more crappy reviews, you mean?'

'Bit touchy today, are we? One bad review from a dickhead doesn't mean a thing.'

'A dickhead who happens to be one of the country's leading critics.'

'Don't take it to heart so. There'll be good notices for Born and Bled. It's a terrific book. It'll do well.'

'Hmmm.'

'Stop worrying about it and think about the next one.'

'I have thought about it. You've got the outline.'

'Yeah ... '

'And?'

'At a time like this, with your contract up for renewal, we've got to go out with as strong a proposal as –'

'You're saying you don't like it.'

'I'm *not* saying that, Ivor. But you know the state of the industry at the moment, and how picky the publishers are getting.'

'Doesn't my sales record stand for anything?'

'Of course it does. Though you have to admit there was a bit of a decline over your last couple of books. Which is probably to do with the general state of things,' she added quickly, 'rather than any reflection on you. But it's not what you've done in the past that interests them, it's what you're likely to achieve in future. It's all about the numbers.'

'What about loyalty?'

She snorted. 'Oh, dear boy. You do make me laugh. It only works one way in this business. You know that.'

'Silly of me.'

'So you can see why the outline for the new book's so important. How long do you think it'll take you to… sharpen it up a bit?'

'I don't know that it needs *sharpening up.*'

'*Ivor.*' Her no nonsense voice now. 'I'm your agent. Listen to me.'

He sighed. 'All right. I'll take a look at it. Give me a couple of days.'

'Good. By the way, have you come up with a title yet?'

'Cat's Got Your Tongue. Seeing as it's set in a zoo.'

'That could work.' She mulled it over for a few seconds. 'Yeah, I like it. Look, I've got to go. I'll set up a meeting with your editor for later in the week. Meantime, make that outline as grabby as you can. And don't insult any more critics!'

The call further dampened Drummond's already moist spirits. He tried to put it out of his mind and focus on reworking the outline, though he didn't see the need.

He found it difficult to concentrate at first. But as he went through what he'd written he began to think that perhaps it *could* be a bit tighter, and a little clearer in places. And the plot lacked a certain vitality, if he were being honest. He set to putting it right. After a couple of hours the narrative was in better shape and the rough edges had been smoothed. He even added an idea or two that had just occurred to him. At which point he was sufficiently moved to try for a first draft of the opening chapter, and maybe the one after.

The day went by. He worked steadily, pausing only for strong coffee and the occasional cigarette. Smoking he restricted to the garden, a feeble way of kidding himself that it was a step towards kicking the filthy habit. But the two or three times he was out there he couldn't wait to get back to his desk, which had to be a good sign.

By late afternoon most of his head was in bookland. If he hadn't quite got into that state of transcendence that comes when a writer truly engages with what they're writing, he was very close.

He cried out.

The stab of pain in his right leg was that sharp. A hot dagger twisting in his thigh.

Drummond stood up, or tried to. He nearly fell. His leg gave a stinging flare, and it lacked the strength to support him. He slumped back into his chair, and sat there for ten minutes or more, until suffering dropped to mere discomfort and he dared try again. This time he made it to the couch in the living room.

In his pocket he found the strip of pain killers from yesterday. He took two, dry, not wanting to face a hobble to the kitchen. The pain nagged for another hour, then began to diminish. Night fell, the room darkened.

The phone rang. He thought about not answering, but gave in.

It was Clarrie. Never at rest.

'You're booked for the publisher meet at three the day after tomorrow at their offices,' she announced crisply. 'How's the outline going?'

'I've had a good day.' He regarded his propped leg. 'Well, apart from the beginning and the end of it.'

'What? Are you still dwelling on that idiot critic?'

'No, I didn't mean that. I – It doesn't matter. So, who pitches this new proposal at the meeting, you or me?'

'Ah, yes, that's another thing.'

'You sound awkward, Clarrie. That's not like you.'

'It's this way, my dear –'

'You're not going to be there, are you?'

'I'm *so* sorry, darling. I'd *love* to be there, you know that. But of all my clients I *know* you're the one who can be totally relied on to sell an idea.' The stony voice appeared. 'Just don't talk business with them. That's strictly my department.'

'I'd feel better if you were there, Clarrie.'

'And I *should* be. Absolutely. Unfortunately I have another appointment that clashes and I absolutely must –'

'Who with?'

'Oh, you know…'

'Another client?'

'Ben Diamond, if you must know.'

'I see.' His tone was cool.

'Now, Ivor, you're not going to be silly about this, are you? You're perfectly capable of handling that meeting by yourself. And I do have other clients, you know.'

'I understand, Clarrie. You'd prefer to be with one of your new young wunderkinds.'

'Three o'clock,' she repeated, 'the day after tomorrow,' and hung up.

He made his way back to his workroom. The pain was still there but barely noticeable. Glutted with writing, he went on the net.

A comment thread had opened up under his blog about Bradshaw. As far as he could see, most of the messages agreed with what he said about the critic. But that was only to be expected of hardcore fans who went to the trouble of registering in the first place. A few were cautious about his decision to respond to the review. One posting, from someone whose user name meant nothing to him, simply said, *Another review*, followed by a link. Drummond hesitated for a moment, then clicked on it.

He landed in a prestigious literary site, and an appraisal of *Born and Bled* by a reviewer he'd vaguely heard of. Another bad review. Not as vitriolic as the one in *The Times*, but definitely waspish. It spoke of structural faults, flimsiness, disappointment.

Drummond noticed that the review was put up at 5.10pm. The same time he'd felt the pain. He remembered looking at the wall clock in his workroom as he ineffectually massaged his leg.

On the principle that part of a writer's necessary armoury is a thick skin, he tried to mentally put the review aside, much as it rankled. The juxtaposition of timing was curious but no more than a fluke, he decided.

He checked his email. The inbox rapidly filled with messages from gambling sites, promises of millions from Nigeria and offers to enlarge his penis. He went through deleting them with a zeal he'd like to apply to certain book reviewers. The roughly ten per cent of remaining messages were genuine and needed his attention. He couldn't face them. Instead, he brought up the daily book trade news alert he subscribed to, which had been sent about thirty minutes earlier. He scanned the list of headlines. The third stopped him dead.

LEADING CRITIC IN BIZARRE ACCIDENT

Beneath was a photograph of Philip Bradshaw.

The accompanying text was brief. Bradshaw had been on a junket the previous day, one of a group of journalists visiting a printing company's revamped works. The tour included the unveiling of a newly-installed electric guillotine, a heavy duty piece of equipment capable of slicing through waist-high stacks of paper. Although supposedly dormant, somehow the machine had unexpectedly activated as Bradshaw was inspecting the blades. His right hand had been severed.

Expressing his "extreme regret" at the tragedy, the plant manager was quoted as saying that the reason for the accident was currently a mystery. Bradshaw's condition was said to be "serious but not life threatening."

What Drummond couldn't get out of his head was what he'd written in his blog. The bit about wishing for something that stilled Bradshaw's hand.

He grew less fond of the centre of town every time he went there, which these days was as infrequently as possible. But it was a long-standing, regular arrangement, and the easiest place to reach for him and the two people he was going to meet.

For someone used to working in isolation the crowds seemed overwhelming. Drummond, the typical control freak writer, also had an uncomfortable feeling that if he told these people what to do they wouldn't obey him. Not that his characters always did either, come to think of it.

For all their buzz and bustle, his surroundings weren't as distracting as his thoughts. He was pondering yesterday's flurry of odd events. Clarrie heard the news about Bradshaw too, and had given Drummond a late call. They mouthed faux sympathy over the accident, though their shock was real enough. She referred to life mirroring Drummond's blog; all the more reason not to harass critics, she said. But she hadn't made a connection about the hand, just him wishing Bradshaw ill. He came close to telling her about... About what? A couple of unrelated pains? Coincidences involving time? He judged it wiser to say nothing.

His reverie dissipated when he arrived at the wine bar. The place had an unreconstituted 1980's look; cutesy latticed windows on the outside, red leather chairs and soft tawny lighting within. The bar was crowded, yet he had no trouble spotting one of the people he was looking for.

Elizabeth Rivers had the sort of personality, and dress sense, that made her hard to miss. A woman of a certain age, which was to say past forty, she had flaming red hair and was fashionably dressed. She was a novelist. Decidedly not chick lit, she insisted, though that's essentially what she was. And successful enough that, for Betty, it was always Gucci everything.

'Ivor, darling!' she boomed, turning heads her way. She hugged him. They air kissed.

After exchanging pleasantries, and agreeing for the umpteenth time that they really should change the venue for these meetings, he asked whether she'd received the copy of *Born and Bled* he had his publisher send her.

'Yes, darling. Thank you.'

'And... have you had a chance to read it?'

'Frankly, no. I'm too busy writing my own stuff, and it's just not my kind of thing.' She laughed, not unkindly. 'I tell you this every time, Ivor.'

He should have known better. While appreciating her honesty, he felt frustrated. With two negative reviews in so far he wanted *her* opinion, which he suspected would have been more incisive than her manner might suggest. Under the tan, bling and designer labels, Betty ran deep.

'That's all right,' he said, hiding his disappointment.

'It'll be a huge success, Ivor, whether I read it or not. And one you deserve.' She raised her glass to him.

Unlike some people he could think of, he knew she meant what she said. That was one of the reasons he liked her.

Rashly, he pushed it. 'I was hoping you might have made an exception this time.'

'Would you read *mine*? No, of course you wouldn't. That's why you don't get little packages from *my* publisher. But why are you so anxious that I should read this one?'

'Not *anxious*. It's just… the reviews. There haven't been many so far, but they've not been good.'

'Like Philip Bradshaw's, you mean?'

'Oh, so you read *that*.'

'I'm not completely indifferent to what's happening to my friends, Ivor. Sure, the review was mean-spirited, but why worry about it? We've all had plenty of bad notices. We get over them. And you know those people set out to wound.' Her face took on the look that signalled gossip or news or scandal to pick over. 'And talking of wounding, what about that accident Bradshaw had? *Horrible.*'

'Yes.'

'So perhaps you should keep that in mind.'

'What do you mean?'

'If you think badly of him. After what the poor man's been through and everything.'

'Oh, right.' Betty had made no reference to the coincidence about the hand. Apparently she hadn't read his blog, unsurprisingly.

'Look,' she said, 'if it's so important to you, I'll read your book.'

'No. Please. Don't bother.'

'I've offended you.'

'No, no! Absolutely not. You couldn't offend me, Betty. You just made me realise I've been worrying about it too much.' He wished he had his fingers crossed.

'Well, the offer's there. And if you ever - Oh, look. There's Bob.' She waved. *'Oooeeee!'* Heads turned again.

Bob Parker approached grinning. He was the youngest of the trio, and grey hairs were just a rumour as far as his unruly mop of sandy locks was concerned. Bob looked well enough, except for the slight premature stoop and pallid complexion that spoke of his profession. He wrote books in the same genre as Drummond's, crime thrillers, although quite different in style, and had once been a kind of protégé.

Parker's first priority, once greetings were done, was fetching drinks. House wine for him and Drummond, another of whatever expensive tipple Betty was having.

No sooner had he placed their glasses on the wobbly, mock antique table than he brought up the subject of the accident. 'What about Bradshaw, then? Losing a hand like that. *Nasty.*' He took a sip of his drink. 'Mind you, after that review he wrote I doubt you're too cut up about it, Ivor. Unlike Bradshaw.'

'Bob!,' Betty remonstrated, giving him a reproachful look. 'Bad taste.'

'Well, he can be a spiteful little bugger. I'm not going to be a hypocrite and pretend I'm devastated because of what happened. His reviews are often bloody hurtful.'

Drummond reflected on how, in a funny kind of way, that was truer than he knew.

He'd arranged for a copy of *Born and Bled* to be sent to Parker too, and was going to ask if he'd read it. But as Bob hadn't already volunteered an opinion he decided against saying anything. Maybe he hadn't had the chance to read the book. Worse, perhaps he had.

Unlike Drummond, Bob Parker had one of his novels adapted for television, which, if he was being honest, Drummond had been a little envious about. The fact that the adaptation was generally agreed to be poor somewhat alleviated the feeling. Parker survived the setback. None of his subsequent books had been adapted, but they remained popular. However, the subject was still raw and the others learned to avoid it.

The conversation drifted away from Bradshaw, to Ivor's relief, and settled on industry chitchat. They swapped rumours, and indulged in a bit of character assassination, while keeping themselves well-lubricated. Normally, Drummond enjoyed these get-togethers, and always kept a place in his diary for them. But he wasn't really engaged. Too much else occupied him.

Betty was relating an unflattering anecdote about a rival. '...and then she had the nerve to claim it wasn't plagiarism at all but –'

'*Ouch!*'

'Ivor? What's the matter?'

'Nothing. Just a... a shooting pain, in my ankle.'

'You okay?' Bob asked.

'I'm fine.' He wasn't, but didn't need a fuss.

'Sure?' Betty said. 'You look pale.'

'I'm all right. It's just something trivial, like... RSI.'

'Only if you type with your feet,' Bob offered.

'You know what I mean; something minor. Really, it's nothing.'

'How is it now?' Betty wanted to know.

'Just a twinge,' he informed her feebly. In fact his ankle burned, and he tried not to fidget.

They talked on after that, although desultorily, and he pretended he wasn't hurting. By the time they called it quits the pain had died down enough for him to shuffle to the door. Bob offered to see him home. He politely turned him down, and watched as Bob and Betty went their separate ways.

He gasped. Another pain hit, in his shoulder. As though someone had thumped him with a ball hammer. He steadied himself against a wall and took a breath.

Eventually, he caught a taxi.

The journey home was uncomfortable. But on the way his ankle and shoulder eased.

There was a heap of post on the mat. He scooped it up and dropped it on the living room table. Deciding to run a bath, he went through and turned on the taps. While it filled he looked at the post. Most was junk. But there was also a shrink-wrapped copy of *Remit* magazine with his name on the cover. This issue carried a short story he'd written. He'd forgotten about that. He wrote few shorts, unless he had a particularly good idea, and only submitted this one because of *Remit's* standing. That was at least six months ago.

Something occurred to him. He went to his workroom. Online, he looked at several sites that might have reviewed the issue. Two had. Neither was particularly complimentary about his story. They had been put up at just about the same time he felt the ankle and shoulder pains, both of which had all but gone now. He had the crazy idea that he got lesser, shorter-lived pains for short stories than novels.

From the corner of his eye he saw movement. Water was seeping from under the bathroom door. The forgotten bath had overflowed.

Cleaning up the mess hardly improved his mood. Early as it was, he called it a night and went to bed.

Sleep was hard.

The doctor was reassuringly silver-haired, bespectacled and white-coated.

He leaned back in his chair, fingers steepled. 'We've run virtually every test there is, Mister Drummond. Your blood pressure, heart, lungs, reflexes, you name it. Everything appears perfectly normal.' He indicated the X-rays on a wall-mounted light box. 'And these confirm no internal abnormalities.'

'Well, that's good news, I suppose.'

'In the sense that we can find nothing physically wrong with you, yes, it is. But we still have no explanation for the pains you say you suffered.'

'They were real enough.'

'I don't doubt it. But there's a puzzle about the range of symptoms you reported.' He glanced down at his notes. 'Bad headache, leg, ankle and shoulder pains. You've also had trouble sleeping.'

'That's right.' Drummond had told him about the pains, but held back on mentioning the other, weird stuff. He didn't want to be diagnosed as cracking-up.

'It's quite a spread, and no one condition is likely to manifest in such diverse ways. At least, none that showed up in the tests.'

'So what do you think this is?'

'Is your job particularly stressful, Mister Drummond?'

'It has its strains. I don't know if it's worse than any other profession.'

'I imagine a writer's life could be rather... demanding. Perhaps even more so for a successful writer.'

'Sometimes.'

'A somewhat tenuous existence too, I should think, with everything depending on the fortunes of each book.'

'They say you're only as good as your last one,' Drummond admitted.

'And should something you've written be greeted with less than enthusiasm —'

'What are you getting at, Doctor?'

'I'm a bit of a reader myself, and I like to keep up with the literary scene, so to speak.'

Oh, no, Drummond assumed with weary familiarity. *He's written a book and wants tips on getting published.*

'Consequently I tend to read reviews a lot,' the doctor continued, 'and I couldn't help but notice that your new book –'

'What exactly has this to do with your medical opinion?'

'Simply that I can understand the effect such reviews might have. Tell me, Mister Drummond –'

Here it comes, Drummond thought.

'– do you think you might be depressed?'

'No, I don't.'

'Depression is very prevalent among writers.'

'And doctors, I believe.'

The doctor looked flummoxed for a moment, then ploughed on. 'Given that your assortment of symptoms seems almost random, we have to consider whether there's a psychosomatic element involved.'

'You think I'm making them up.'

'Absolutely not! But the mind can play some nasty tricks, particularly when under pressure.'

Drummond wanted to protest, but he couldn't be bothered. He let it all wash over him, and left with a prescription for tranquillisers, which he tossed into a waste bin in the street. Then he made for the nearest underground station.

Naturally there were no free seats and he had to stand. As usual, the carriage was crammed with stony-faced commuters avoiding eye contact. The only exceptions were a couple of people who might have been deranged, although that was moot. There was a time when someone talking to themselves in public was a giveaway. With the advent of hands-free mobiles it became hard to tell. He adopted his tube survival persona. The one where you try to look like you could be the nut with a cleaver.

About halfway home he felt the first pangs of something like indigestion. His discomfort quickly grew. He had a pain in his guts and fiery bile in his mouth. Cold sweat dappled his forehead. The train pulled into a station and he decided to get off. Other passengers studiously ignored him as he elbowed his way out.

He sat on a platform bench, trying not to vomit. After what

seemed lages the pain dimmed and he felt well enough to resume his journey.

Arriving home, he found a copy of the evening paper crammed into his letterbox. It contained another less than enthusiastic review of *Born and Bled.*

Work didn't go well for the rest of the day. A long time passed before he managed to sleep that night.

He woke in the small hours with an excruciating cramp in his legs. Eventually he got up, went to his study and trawled the net. Another review. Not good. He began to wish he hadn't thrown away the tranx prescription, and made do with alcohol.

Being an inveterate list-maker he'd noted the names of the critics who displeased him. Going through, he wrote rebuffs of most of the bad reviews he'd had. He didn't restrain himself, or stick to purely literary arguments; he lambasted the people who wrote them. Working with a passion, he damned their reputations and blackened their names, accusing them of heinous crimes, and not only against literature. Minors, household appliances and farmyard animals featured. Remembering Bradshaw, in each case he ended with a wish that the subject of his displeasure suffer some kind of injury. He was quite imaginative in that respect.

Dawn was breaking before he finished. Mindful of the promise he'd made to Clarrie, he didn't post what he'd written online. Besides, he could do without a dozen writs for libel. He wasn't that crazy. He was just getting it out of his system, he told himself.

Needing *some* sleep, he forced himself back to bed. He was due at the meeting with his publisher in a matter of hours.

Drummond braved the hated tube again, and with even less enthusiasm after yesterday's unpleasantness. The overcrowding, the stifling air, the body odour; all combined to remind him of his last trip.

With relief he arrived at his stop in the centre of town. Glancing down the crowded platform he noticed a pair of familiar figures getting off the same train, several carriages along. Walking with their backs to him they looked like the number 10. The younger was tall and lean, the other at least a head shorter and squat. "1" was dressed smart casual. "0" was slightly more formal in a dark suit, albeit shabby. Both wore glasses.

His editor and his publisher. Small world.

The tube was a great leveller. The impossibility of driving in the city, or being driven, meant even the pampered had to use it.

Drummond looked at his watch. If they were heading for the office at this time they must be coming back from lunch. Which dashed any hope of them buying his, and a meeting over lunch trumped a meeting without lunch, status-wise.

He let them get ahead, and soon they were lost in the throng. Their offices were nearby and he had plenty of time before the meeting.

Two bookshops survived in the area. He visited both. Neither was exactly bustling. Several of the few browsers he saw were taking notes, presumably so they could buy cheaper on the Internet.

He checked for copies of *Born and Bled*. Were they not quite as well displayed as his earlier books? Were there fewer copies in those piles than previously? Did that mean it was selling or that the shop's order was low? He didn't have time to introduce himself to the staff and ask how it was going. Instead, he engaged in the age-old author pastime of making sure his books were face-front.

A few minutes later he stood before a white stone, brutalist office block. Above the immense glass frontage a sign read:

Savage & Darke : Publishers

Once a venerable company, now an outpost of a mighty international conglomerate.

He stepped inside to be confronted by the most powerful people in publishing. But he got past the receptionists without too much trouble and took the lift.

The doors slid open in the upper reaches. Plusher carpets

and another receptionist. But whereas the ones downstairs were valkyries, she was a coiffured ninja. The last line of defence. Her well-manicured fingers played over the keys of an internal phone. He was announced, and asked to wait.

Drummond parked himself in one of the humiliatingly low chairs, abutted by equally stumpy glass tables scattered with fashionable magazines he hadn't heard of. Three walls of the large reception area were honeycombed with pigeonholes displaying copies of current books. Where was his? The ninja interrupted before he finished checking, and he was ushered into the presence.

His editor, Trevor Thompson, greeted him first. He said good afternoon. On past evidence that was probably a lie. Thompson's boss, Publishing Director Martin Egger, delivered a clammy handshake. Coffee was offered, Drummond refused, and they settled around Egger's imposing desk.

Drummond noticed a flicker of eye contact between superior and underling. The message conveyed was *You do most of the talking.*

'So, Ivor,' Thompson began, 'you're going to run us through what you hope to write next.'

Drummond noted the use of *hope*. Or was he reading too much into it? 'Just the basic outline. I've got the full proposal here, along with a couple of sample chapters.' He nodded at the briefcase he'd brought.

'The essentials are all we need for now.'

'Right.' He cleared his throat. 'Well, the story centres on a zoological research institute where...'

He talked them through the plot, leaving out extraneous detail and highlighting what he hoped were its unexpected twists. Gauging the reaction of his little audience was difficult. Egger, who scribbled the occasional note, was a famously cold fish and particularly difficult to read. Thompson attempted various facial expressions, with mixed results.

All the while, Drummond worried that at any moment he

might be hit by some unsuspected ailment. But he finished unscathed.

They complimented him while managing not to voice an actual opinion. At least neither of them used the word 'interesting'. Otherwise, they made all the right noises, wore the rictus smiles.

'We'll be in touch with your agent,' Eggers promised.

'We've just seen Clarrie, actually,' Thompson dropped.

'Really?' Drummond said.

'Yes, over lunch. With Ben Diamond.'

'We're very excited about his potential,' Eggers put in.

Thompson nodded. 'The perfect author.'

'In what way?' Drummond asked.

His editor counted off on his fingers. 'He's young, he's very photogenic, he can express himself, he lives here in town.' He clasped his last finger triumphantly, heralding the killer point. 'And after seventeen continuous weeks on a TV reality show he's got a high public profile.'

'You haven't mentioned whether he can write.'

'Oh, we can sort *that* out.'

'By bringing in a real writer.'

'Exactly. Organising the product's no problem.'

Drummond wondered what the going rate was for ghosted… product.

Later, at home, he had a few more aches and pains, though nothing too serious. Capsules reviews, he assumed. But there was also a kind of itching, pins and needles sensation in various parts of his body, and that was beginning to irritate him. He went online, as much to distract himself as anything else.

Before long he found a couple of mildly bad reviews. There were good ones too, of course, adding to some others he'd seen recently. Being a writer, with a writer's anxieties, he tended to discount those.

He momentarily wondered if the good ones counteracted

the bad ones to some degree. Then he considered the possibility that he was going bonkers. He decided he wasn't. Which presumably was exactly what an insane person would think.

The damned itchy, tingling feeling had become annoying. He thought about checking the bathroom cabinet to see if he had some kind of salve.

The phone rang.

'Hello, Ivor? It's Betty.'

'Hi, Betty. How are you?'

'Fine. More to the point, how are *you*? You looked pretty rough when we parted the day before yesterday.'

'I'm fine.'

'Sure?'

'Really.' He was massaging the prickling in his chest. 'But it's sweet of you to ask.'

'Okay. Just checking. I saw Bob today. He sends his best.'

'He came to your place?'

'No, I dropped in on him. I don't think he feels too comfortable visiting my neck of the woods. Seems to bring back his student radicalism. They're posh round my way, you see. If there was a riot they'd throw Molotov aperitifs.'

'I meant to ask him if he was working on anything.'

'He'd obviously been writing. Solitaire was still on his PC screen.'

'You're talking to the south-east regional champion.'

'We all procrastinate, Ivor. Anyway, he told me a piece of news I hadn't picked up on. I wonder if you've heard. About Michael Wheaton.'

Drummond felt a pang of apprehension.

'You know, the critic on the Gazette,' she added. 'Gave your new book a bit of a drubbing.'

'Yes, yes. I know. What about him?'

'Seems he got himself involved in a fight of some kind, in a bar. *And* came out the worst. Some drunk broke his nose.'

That floored him. All he could say was, 'Oh.'

'Another one bites the dust.'

'Sorry?'

'Well, it looks like whenever someone writes a bad review of your book there's a comeback. You're not practising voodoo are you, Ivor?' She laughed.

He joined in, weakly.

As soon as the call was over he got straight back on the net. He had no trouble finding a news item about Wheaton that confirmed what Betty told him. According to the report, Wheaton had got involved in an argument with somebody who ended up thrashing him.

Drummond checked several other critics' names. He came up with stories involving a bicycle accident, a tumble down a flight of concrete steps, a scalding, and a savaging by a stray dog. As far as he could make out, no one had linked this string of mishaps befalling the literary establishment.

He was shaken. Every one of the incidents mirrored exactly what he'd written in the last batch of rebuttals. Somebody was going to see the connection – all the injured critics had bad reviews of *Born and Bled* in common – and that could implicate him. Although he couldn't see how anything could be proven.

Then he remembered. He had written those things but not posted them online. The files still sat in his PC, but what he wished on his tormentors had happened anyway.

He wouldn't have slept in any event, even without the itchiness.

The next morning saw him in an irritable mood. He was tired after a tortured night, and the tingling had gone up a notch or two, with occasional spasms thrown in.

Doing his best to ignore the discomfort, he took to the net and looked up the remaining critics he'd laid into. He drew a blank on several of the lesser names. Presumably they didn't warrant coverage, assuming anything bad had happened to them. But he found news items on three others. One was struck a glancing blow by a falling tile, another collided with a teenager on a skateboard, the third had somehow driven into a canal. All exactly as he'd... predicted? Was that the right word? Wasn't *made happen* more accurate?

And just by writing down his malicious thoughts.

He couldn't concentrate, couldn't make sense of it all. The pins and needles had given way to multiple minor pains, like a host of tiny insect bites all over his body.

Something terrible occurred to him.

Pounding his keyboard hard enough to shake the desk, he investigated. His fear was confirmed.

Comments about his current book were being posted on Twitter. Ivor Drummond was trending.

Each negative tweet was a little barb, a hot spike aggravating his flesh. He felt near maddened by it, and close to being sick. Sweat-drenched, it was all he could do to jot down the names of the most spiteful.

He thought about calling his doctor, but quickly decided against it. The last thing he needed was to be told it was all in his mind.

So he went back to bed and stayed there.

He didn't know how he got through the following twenty four hours.

By mid-morning the stinging pains that plagued him slowly subsided. He guessed the limit of attention spans had been reached and the mob had moved on to hound somebody else.

Just after lunch his agent called.

'They've come through with a decision about Cat's Got Your Tongue,' Clarrie said.

'That was quick.'

'Quick isn't always good, Igor. They've decided to pass on it. I'm sorry. I think they'd probably already made up their minds to reject even before you met with them.'

'So why couldn't they have said that at the time?'

'To your face? *Please*, darling.'

'What happens now? Do we go back to them with a reworked proposal, or something new?'

'Forget Savage and Darke. They think you'd be better served by a different publisher.'

'I see.'

'Don't be downhearted, darling. They're not the only house in town. I'll be getting straight to work on finding a new home for you.'

'Thanks, Clarrie.'

'But do bear in mind that things are tough at the moment, and I won't pretend that once word gets round that S and D have let you go - '

'Yeah, yeah. I know.'

'Sorry to be the bearer of bad news. Chin up. I'll be in touch.'

So that was it. The abrupt end to a long-running relationship, and not with a bang. Not with anything much at all, in fact. No bottle of scotch or bouquet delivered. Not even an email saying *Thanks for all the money you made us. Good luck in future.* Nothing. Fuck all.

Drummond recalled a piece of advice an old writer of his acquaintance had once offered him about the industry. *These people are not your friends,* he said. *You simply have a business relationship with them. Never forget that.*

A couple of hours later he got a nasty pain in his back. As though someone had plunged a knife between his shoulder-blades. He had no need to look for its source.

That decided him.

A lot of inventive ideas had come to him during his restless night, including a particularly colourful one concerning the tube.

He had his list. That and his writing ability was all he needed.

A large drink to hand, he began working on the first obituary.

About The Author

Stan Nicholls is the author of more than thirty books, most of them in the fantasy and science fiction genres, for both adult and young readers. Titles include *Strange Invaders*, *Fade to Black*, *The Nightshade Chronicles* trilogy and *Wordsmiths of Wonder: Fifty Interviews With Writers of the Fantastic*. He adapted David Gemmell's *Legend* and *Wolf in Shadow* into graphic novel form, novelised TV series *Dark Skies*, and wrote authorised biographies of, among others, Gerry Anderson of *Thunderbirds* fame and *Coronation Street's* Willam Roache. His Quicksilver trilogy (Dreamtime trilogy in the US) - *Quicksilver Rising, Quicksilver Zenith* and *Quicksilver Twilight* - is published in the UK by Voyager/HarperCollins.

His Orcs: First Blood trilogy - *Bodyguard of Lightning, Legion of Thunder* and *Warriors of the Tempest* - published in the UK by Gollancz, is a worldwide bestseller, with over a million copies sold to date. The associated Orcs story 'The Taking' was shortlisted for the 2001 British Fantasy Award. The second trilogy, Orcs: Bad Blood, consists of *Weapons of Magical Destruction, Army of Shadows* and *Inferno*. The trilogies have appeared as unexpurgated audiobooks, read by John Lee and published by Tantor Media. An original Orcs graphic novel, *Orcs: Forged For War*, illustrated by Joe Flood, was published in October 2011 by First Second Books in the US, Pan Macmillan in the UK and Les Editions Gallimard in France, and entered the *New York Times* bestseller list. It also won the 2011 Geek Life Award for Best Comic Book of the Year, and was awarded a Great GN Accolade by *Graphic Novel Reporter*.

His books have been published in more than 20 countries, including Argentina, Australia, Brazil, Bulgaria, Canada, China, Czech Republic, France, Germany, Holland, Italy, New Zealand,

Poland, Romania, Russia, Spain and the United States.

Before taking up writing full-time in 1981, Stan co-owned and managed Notting Hill bookstore Bookends, and was manager of specialist sf bookshop Dark They Were and Golden Eyed. He was the first manager of Forbidden Planet's original London store, and helped establish and run the New York branch.

A journalist for national and specialist publications, and the Internet, he was for six years the science fiction and fantasy book reviewer for London listings magazine *Time Out*, and subsequently reviewed popular science titles for the magazine. His journalism has appeared in *The Guardian, The Independent, The Times, Film Monthly, Films & Filming, Movie, Rock Power, SFX, Sight & Sound* and some seventy other publications. He has had approximately fifty short stories published in anthologies and magazines.

He was the recipient of *Le'Fantastique Lifetime Achievement Award for Contributions to Literature,* presented at the Trolls & Legendes Festival in Mons, Belgium, 7th-8th April 2007. Stan is Chair of the annual David Gemmell Awards For Fantasy. The first presentation, which he co-hosted, took place at the headquarters of The Magic Circle in London on 19th June 2009.

Stan is married to psychotherapist Anne Nicholls, who writes self-help books and journalism under that name, and sf/fantasy as Anne Gay.

www.stannicholls.com